THE UNDERTAKER AND HIS DOG

Copyright © 2025 by Raven De Cervantes
All rights reserved.

No part of this book may be reproduced in any form or by any electronic or mechanical means, including information storage and retrieval systems, without written permission from the author, except for the use of brief quotations in a book review.

This book is a work of fiction. Any reference to real events, people, or places are used fictitiously. Other names, characters, places and incidents are the products of the author's imagination. Any resemblance to actual events, locales, or persons; living or dead, is entirely coincidental.

THE UNDERTAKER AND HIS DOG

RAVEN DE CERVANTES

(Heritage Images)

For my souldog Bruno, gone but never forgotten.

INTRODUCTION

Among the misty English mornings there was an undertaker and his beloved companion. Every day they set off in the old hearse. They rumbled down twisted country lanes, and back again in time for tea. They'd return to their cozy cottage in the valley; where the sheep would come down from the crags, and they'd amble over to baa their regards. Their woolen faces partially hidden behind the mossy stone walls. The familiar, but doddering cottage door would welcome them with creaky hinges, and they'd finally settle into the warmth of their quaint English home. A fire crackled on in the hearth, as it sang them to sleep. This was the life of Ernest and Wilbur, until one day it wasn't...

CHAPTER ONE

The cottage door moaned like an elderly man as it opened into the damp English morning, Ernest adjusted his flat cap and let out a shrill whistle that echoed through the dawning valley. He turned his gaze to the thick fog gathering at the tops of the hills and he could only hope it would clear for their drive. As he neared the old hearse, a beautiful black and white border collie came bounding up from the fields in all of his fluffy glory. Ernest smiled as he leaned down to stroke Wilbur's slightly wet head. He stared into his best friend's soft caramel-colored eyes. Wilbur stared back at him turning his head with his wonky ears, one up and one down. Ernest gave a thoughtful chuckle as he bent to give his friend some well-deserved scratches. Clearly satisfied with their morning routine being completed, Wilbur ran around to take his place on the passenger's side of the hearse.

"We've got four bodies to deliver old boy. A bit of a shorter one today, but it looks like we are starting up north." Ernest turned again toward the fog rolling slowly in, he shook his head and shuffled into his seat. He reached over with a groan to open the door for Wilbur who happily climbed in. Ernest adjusted himself behind the steering wheel, and with a good crank of the keys, the old hearse rumbled to a start. The windshield wipers came to life with much complaint as they made their first squeaky trek across the glass. Ernest turned the dial on the radio until he found a station that came through clearly. He and Wilbur listened intently and sang along loudly as they did on almost every workday.

"Not sure how you always seem to have better pitch than me Wilbs." Ernest flashed his friend a smile and patted him on the back. Wilbur barked pridefully in return. It was some time before they finally arrived at Winston's Care Home. A man named Sam needed to get to the morgue, and quickly. He was a soldier who'd fallen in the war. His body had been flown in specially from Germany. Ernest sighed, mostly at the thought of another young man taken too soon, and partly because he was nervous. He knew this needed to go very smoothly. Soldier burials were always treated with utmost respect and punctuality. He took a deep breath as he pulled into a space labeled "Rose Garden." He knew this was the right spot. He turned to Wilbur with a stressful grin, Wilbur only looked back in confidence and gave him a reassuring grumble.

"Right, thank you. You always know what to say. I'll be back!" Ernest breathed deeply once more and climbed out of the hearse. Wilbur patiently waited and started to close his eyes. He liked that Ernest was the one who took care of the dead. He couldn't think of a more understanding man to do such a job. It took a lot of compassion and strength in more ways than one, and his friend had it in spades. Wilbur sighed contentedly at the thought of his life; long trips, naps, plenty of time outside, and what's more the company of a brilliant companion. They were truly inseparable, and Wilbur was grateful. The smell of coming Spring crept through the hearse windows, it mingled with the old leather scent of the seats. Wilbur felt as though he was being lulled to sleep. Just as he dozed off, Ernest returned, lumbering out of the care home with huffs and puffs. He loaded Sam as gently as he could into the boot. A large thump shook the hearse. An apology and a sigh followed from Ernest as he wiped the sweat from his brow.

"Right, we've done it. You'll be okay now Sam. Wilbur and I will look after you." He gave the temporary casket a few loving taps and shut the boot carefully. As he opened the driver's side door Wilbur looked at him thoughtfully through sleepy eyes. "This second war is proving to be even worse than the first. Count yourself lucky to be a dog these days Wilbs. You get to return home every day, and to a warm fire as well, not a care in the world.... Well I suppose I'm lucky too. We just need to make sure we're taking extra care of these poor young men." Ernest gave his best friend a sad smile and another scratch. He adjusted himself in his seat one last time. Wilbur wagged his tail and sighed. Within minutes he was down for a nap as they began their journey north. The next stop was Carlisle, not too far from the Scottish border. The hazy sun began to make a slow exit and sheets of rain started to batter the hearse from all sides. Ernest tightened his grip on the wheel, and his jaw clenched at the thought that the roads would only get narrower. As Ernest anxiously navigated the snaking country lanes, Wilbur snored soundly. Ernest kept his eyes focused ahead. The man on the radio became a soft muffle as he lowered the volume. The steady pitter-patter of raindrops started to slow, and after what seemed an eternity they subsided altogether. Ernest lightened his grip on the steering wheel and gave a small sigh of relief. He gave the old hearse some throttle, they were starting to fall behind schedule.

Softly, Ernest started singing along to the radio again. He let his gaze wander to the rolling green hills. His favorite part of Spring was counting the lambs in their fields as they drove by. He couldn't help but smile at them hopping and kicking through the wildflowers. His favorite were always the Black Valais, he felt they looked like something from a fantasy story. Suddenly, the hearse started to sputter and snapped Ernest out of his daydreams.. He shook his head at himself as he looked at the needle on the gas gauge, it had dipped below empty. He pulled over to the nearest petrol station. Clunking open the gas tank, he noticed Wilbur stir, but only to adjust and return to his neverending nap. A pleasant-looking man came over and began filling the tank. Ernest gave him a wave and handed him a few shillings. His gaze focused on the field across the road, squinting as he looked out. The fog from earlier had finally found them. It crept menacingly across the roads and blanketed the hedgerows.

"I knew this was coming... shooo, it'll be an interesting drive. " He muttered to himself and shook his head worriedly.

"There's a town near about eight miles down the road! If you have time, you could always wait it out." The station man called over to him. Ernest smiled and gave a nod that meant "thank you", slightly embarrassed that his muttering had been heard. He got back into the hearse quietly shutting the door. Once they had left the petrol station behind, they were at a terrible crawl down a country road for what seemed like a hundred miles. Ernest could hardly see a few meters ahead, and the hedges were near enough to touch on either side. He could tell they were nearing the more mountainous roads, as hedges gave way to trees that now reached out on either side of them. A nervous shiver went up his spine. He brushed it off and tried his best to peer through the fog.

"This is just relentless... I'm going to have to take a turn onto the next side road and wait it out." He whispered partly to himself and partly to his sleeping friend. He looked over and Wilbur was twitching and kicking up a storm. He couldn't help but let out a nervous laugh.

"What are you chasing over there you nitwit? You could sleep through a hurricane. Maybe I'm a little jealous. Ahhh who am I kidding, I could never do this job without you buddy. Sleeping or not." He smiled sweetly and gave Wilbur a few loving strokes. The hearse creaked around the next turn as they came to an even slower pace. "Yeah, think we'll have a quick stop and see if this fog will dissipate. We won't make it alive at this rate. I don't think an undertaker works too well if they're the one needing the undertaking." He joked in a bit of a nervous tone. "You okay with a bit of a break boss?" He jeered at his friend who still dreamed away.

Wilbur only twitched an ear. Ernest just shook his head and stared at his friend. "I'm not sure if you're listening, but I really am lucky to have you Wilbs. You really do make these days a lot easier. We're surrounded by death everyday and yet I have friend who is so full of life... The best friend. Ahh I'm getting all mushy now." He looked at his sleepy friend with unending love, and he meant every word. He loved that silly dog, truly. Ernest took a deep satisfied breath as he swung the old hearse around toward the nearest side street, as he turned his head to look across the road, everything went black. Ernest felt as if he were looking through a telescope as the hearse swerved and skidded across the road. Before he could even blink, he heard Wilbur cry out, he awoke with a fright and clambered across the seat. His nails frantically scraped the seat fabric. They were spinning out of control. They began to slip and slide, a horrible sound screeched out as they whipped around. Ernest saw the faint lights of a big lorry speeding away. He reached out for Wilbur. A loud crash echoed around them, and then all was dark...

AFTER A LONG TIME, ERNEST CAME TO. IN FRONT OF him was a smashed windscreen and a giant yew tree. The hearse's bonnet was almost unrecognizable. It had been crumpled like a tin can. Dazed, he wiped at his nose and small amounts of blood stained the white sleeve of his undershirt. He stared blankly, and then as if a lightning bolt shot through him he remembered Wilbur. He hurriedly scanned his surroundings, but his noble companion was nowhere to be found. Ernest frantically tried to open the driver's side door. Finally, it flung open. He stumbled out and caught his reflection in the cracked side mirror. Just a few cuts and bruises. Taking his tattered handkerchief from his pocket, he wiped the blood away from the gash above his eye and grabbed his jacket from the seat. He shook out the shards of glass and threw it on.

All he cared about was finding Wilbur. He turned for one last look at his hearse smashed into the old tree.

"Good god, Sam..." he remembered quietly as his eyes found the casket in the boot. From what he could see the casket looked to be unharmed. He figured he would sort it out later, first was Wilbur. He observed the land around him, and his heart began to sink. They had crashed in what seemed to be the middle of nowhere. A shaken sigh escaped his lips as he kept walking, somewhat aimlessly. There was no time to lose. He called Wilbur's name over and over. As he walked, the aching in his heart became as heavy as the fog that surrounded him. He headed off into the only forest he could see. Wilbur could be absolutely anywhere by now.

CHAPTER TWO

It was pouring down rain again, and Wilbur had been running for what felt like hours. He wasn't even sure why he was running anymore. He slowed himself down and tried to gather his thoughts. He remembered spinning and a screech that was unbearable. The pain in his front paw reminded him that as he and Ernest crashed, the passenger side window had exploded into thousands of tiny pieces. One of which had found its way into his front paw. He knew he had panicked and he felt ashamed of himself. As he wandered hopelessly in the rain, he couldn't help but feel as though he'd abandoned his best friend. It was as if he couldn't stop himself. As his mind flooded back to the moment that he jumped through that broken window and sprinted into the forest, he could only chalk it down to instincts.

He had only wanted to get away from it all. Now, the only thing he wanted was to find his way back, to find Ernest. But how? By this point he had gotten himself utterly lost. He circled around some trees sniffing heavily at the roots and grass. He headed toward what felt like the right direction. The forest was thick and the spindly branches reached out for him at every turn. His mind was reeling, so much so that it made him feel dizzy. He could only hope that Ernest would forgive him. His frantic heartbeats matched the pace of his steps as he trailed through the brambles with his nose never leaving the ground. The further he walked, the more pain began to emerge throughout his body, the aches crept through his legs and spine in strong pulses, but his determination was stronger.

Wilbur's mind spun through a wheel of thoughts as his paws thudded across the dark forest floor. He thought about the hunger pangs in his stomach and remembered how every Sunday night Ernest would make a roast dinner and give him a bowl with extra gravy, he thought about the warm fire and the comfort of Ernest's lap as his pillow. The rewards of a hard day's work. He wanted it all back, to be home with his best friend, but most of all, he wondered if Ernest was looking for him too. Waves of chilling anxiety washed over him and made his bones tremble. Or was it just the cold? With every thought of Ernest, there was an unshakeable uneasy feeling. It wasn't like him to get himself lost either. He had a keen nose, and usually finding his way around was no big deal.

He prided himself on that, but nothing here smelled right. Every clue was disguised and drenched in rain. Rain mixed with the strangest smell, a smell he couldn't make out no matter how hard he tried. Wilbur winced, the glass in his paw was cutting deeper with every step. Briefly, he caught his bedraggled reflection in a puddle. His white speckled face was now speckled with drops of red as well. His fur was mangled and muddy. His whites became muddled greys and on top of it all he had begun to develop a slight limp. Ultimately, no matter how much he only wanted to keep going, he decided that he should try to take a rest. If only for a few minutes.

After quite some time, he came upon a grove of low-hanging trees and wildflowers. From what he could tell, it smelled safe. As his adrenaline waned, the exhaustion began to consume him. Every one of his bones felt as if they were shivering from the inside, and he was drenched. His paw was throbbing, and the shock was wearing off quickly. His body would thank him for just a minute's sleep, but he hesitated. He knew the low trees would be a good shelter from the rain, and the lush green grass felt comfortable on his aching paws. He circled around a few times as he mulled it over. He tilted his head as what sounded like faint whispers flowed in and out of his ears. He shook it off, he hoped he might just be a bit dazed. Finally, he curled up under the friendliest tree he could find and allowed himself to give in. He made sure the white tip of his tail was visible, in case Ernest found his way to him. Nimbly using his teeth, he tried to dig the glass out of his paw for a while, but soon the weariness was too strong. Wilbur nestled his head into the soft grass and fell into a much-needed sleep. He would continue his search for Ernest as soon as he awoke.

Chapter Three

Ernest gave up his search around midnight. The nearby forest was impossible to navigate with the fog. He hoped that maybe if he took a rest, Wilbur would make his way back. As he slowly walked back to the old hearse, he jolted, remembering Sam again. He ran over and peered through the cracked rear windows. The body and casket looked to be safe and untouched.

"I am so sorry Sam. I will get to a phone tomorrow and get you sorted. You'll be in a nice resting place in no time. Though for tonight, I think we'll have to share the hearse. I'm afraid I don't see anywhere else to sleep." Ernest let out a nervous laugh as he looked around, knowing there was still nothingness around him. He rubbed his forehead. "You'll be taken care of. Just hang in there." He gave Sam a caring nod and made his way to the front end. He laid down his coat on the seat of broken glass. The shards crunched dangerously under his weight, but he fell asleep as quickly as he laid down.

IN THE EARLIEST LIGHT OF DAWN, ERNEST AWOKE and adjusted his flat cap, he shook the glass off of his tweed coat, and headed nervously out in search of the nearest town. He gave a gentle wave as he turned to Sam one more time, trying to tell himself it would all be okay. The dirt of the country road felt harsh under his shoes. He desperately hoped he could find somebody who had seen Wilbur, and a phone. After a fair walk, he came to a lovely countryside village. As he entered the town, he pondered on the fact that he'd never been there before. He was certain he'd been everywhere in England by now. The ancient cobbled streets were inviting, shining with glossy puddles. Within a few minutes, he found a massive dark stone building that read *Lion's Head Inn*. Happily, he spotted a red phone box to the right of it.

Ernest made his way over and phoned the head of the dead. That's what he liked to call him anyways. James was a very nice man, almost too nice. It strangely made Ernest feel even worse, he twirled the phone cord nervously for only a few seconds, until he heard the operator make the connection, and then a friendly voice at the other end.

"Ello?" The West London voice was very familiar and instantly made Ernest feel a bit calmer.

"Hiya James, it's Ernest. I'll just come out with it, Wilbur and I ran into some trouble after picking up Sam."

"Is everyone alright? What happened?"

"As we pulled out of a petrol stop, a thick fog rolled in and I was snaking us along, trying my best to see, but I couldn't shake it. I didn't have a good feeling, so I pulled us over on a side lane in god knows where and one second I was turning to check on Wilbs and the next we were spinning off the road. I saw a mail truck fly by afterward, I'm guessing that's who clipped us. I am so sorry James... The hearse... I don't think she's gonna make it. Sam looks alright, but I won't be able to get him to where he needs to go. I don't know what to do."

"Ern... slow down for me. We can sort it. I'm just glad you two are okay. Wilbur is okay right?" His voice was as gentle as one from London could be.

Ernest paused and swallowed hard trying to keep his eyes from misting over. "Well... The thing is... I don't actually know. He ran off and I haven't found him yet."

"I'm really sorry to hear that Ern, not the news I wanted in the slightest." There was a small silence. "Do you know where you are? I can get the police to go and take care of the hearse and Sam as well." His voice came again, quieter.

"I really have no idea, which is a first for me. The lane I turned down was called Moss Home Lane and we were approaching Lancaster, not sure how far off. The petrol station was called Morrison's and there's an inn here called Lion's Head. I don't see any town info." He explained, trying to peer his head around the phone box.

"Alright, don't worry too much. I'll find it. I'll make a report with the police and they'll see to it. You just worry about finding that dog. He's a good one Ern, and Keep me updated."

"Thanks James. I appreciate you. He really is my best friend, funny how that works. A best friend that can't even speak… I'm rambling now. I'll find him James. I know I will. Thank you again."

"No worries at all Ern. Take as long as you need."

"I will do, thank you. I should go in and find some food. Gather my thoughts."

"No problem. You do what you need to do. Let me know how you're getting on."

Ernest could feel a shared smile and then a faint click as the call ended. He hung the phone back up and stood there for a while, looking at his reflection in the scuffed phone box glass.

Though tattered and worn, Ernest was a handsome-faced man. A reddish tint to his otherwise dark brown curls and beard. He had stormy green eyes that turned almost blue in the rare English sun, and he stood at a rather significant height. He took a deep breath, and removed his flat cap, carefully brushing his hair back with his fingers. Realizing, that it had gotten longer than he thought. He smoothed himself over and tried to look like he hadn't just crawled out of a broken hearse. He took one last look at himself. Then, nervously he made his way into the old inn.

The tears were hard to fight as he desperately pried every man and woman on the whereabouts of his friend. To his dismay, nobody had seen the beautiful border collie. Though everyone said they'd keep a close eye out. Ernest thanked them all and in a saddened daze, he walked to the bar and had a drink to warm his bones. His head sat heavy on his hands. He decided to rent a room and station himself for a while. It would be far better than a glass covered seat in a hearse, and Wilbur had to be around here somewhere.

Eventually, the woman who ran the inn came over, she seemed sweet and she finalized his bill and bookings. She wasted no time getting his room ready for the night and didn't make much conversation. She seemed to understand that he wasn't in the mood to talk. Nonetheless, he thanked her kindly and they shared a vague smile. He slowly walked down the candlelit hall to his new room. As he undressed he looked tiredly into the old victorian mirror. He felt he looked about twenty years older already. Ernest sighed and slowly climbed into the rickety bed. Sleep was not so easily had this time. He tossed and turned, and dreams of Wilbur came like flash floods throughout the night.

The next morning he awoke suddenly and hurried to his feet. Hastily, he got himself dressed and presentable, brushing off the dust and debris from the day before. His clothes were torn and wrinkled, and well-rested he was not, but it didn't matter much. His thoughts were consumed entirely on continuing his search. He splashed his face with some water in the basin near his bed, and quickly walked down the hall, fiddling with his shoes. He grimaced for a second, the uncomfortable bed had come back to bite him.

When he arrived in the tavern, the sun was barely peeking through the fog. There were only a couple of early souls scattered about, struggling through their first cups of tea. He was about to start asking the new faces about Wilbur when he saw that the same woman was tending the bar again. Ernest was slightly taken aback as he took time to notice her in the daylight, she was tall, with brown hair in soft messy ringlets, and golden brown eyes. She had such a soft and kind look about her. He imagined a deer standing in a meadow of wildflowers, he could almost smell the sweet air as she floated between customers. She eventually met his gaze and hurriedly motioned him over. Slightly embarrassed, he approached her, and saw a piece of artwork lying on the bar. Getting closer, he realized it was a drawing of Wilbur, and an uncanny one at that. He looked up at the woman with glassy eyes.

"I decided I would draw him, I hope you don't mind. I thought if you'd like, I could take it down to my uncle's print shop and have some copies stenciled out. We could put them up as lost dog signs. Just sort of an idea I thought of... I know how scared you must be. I just figured somebody needed to do something to help... and... " She stopped herself and shyly twiddled her fingers. She had the loveliest voice. A peaceful haunting song.

Ernest struggled for words. "How did you?"

"Oh sorry, I just overheard you asking about him all night. I felt I couldn't just stand around and do nothing.... I hope I'm not being forward." She blushed nervously.

Ernest shook his head to help ease her. "How did you draw him so well? It looks exactly like him... have you seen him somewhere? Please tell me if you have."

She hesitated. "Well I also overheard you describing him to everyone, and I remember you said he was a border collie. I guess I just tried my best and sketched what came to mind. I'm glad you approve though. I was a bit nervous that I'd be completely off the mark." She smiled a bit less nervously, waiting for him to respond. Ernest studied the drawing, everything was perfect. His soft fluffy hair, the black speckles, his caramel eyes, and the most poignant detail, his lopsided ears. She even captured his smile.

Ernest ran his hand along the drawing. "This is truly remarkable. Thank you. I would love for you to make some signs. I can help you post them around town whenever they're ready... can I have this original one? I can pay you for it."

"Oh don't be silly! Of course, you can have it. I'll go make copies after we close for the day. You can always tag along if you'd like. You can tell me a bit more about Wilbur, and I'm always up for the company." Her voice was comforting.

Ernest politely nodded. He figured some company and some new surroundings couldn't hurt. The woman softly chimed in again. "It breaks my heart really, I know if I were you I would want all the help I could get, so I'll do my best... um...?"

"Ernest, miss." He said kindly.

"Ernest then, you can count on it." She said with an almost knowing smile.

Ernest genuinely returned her smile. He knew he didn't need to say anymore. She turned and floated off toward the kitchens.

"I'll get us a quick snack! You must be starving. Don't go anywhere." She called, playfully attempting to brighten the mood.

Right before she disappeared behind the door, Ernest called out. "Wait! I never got your name!"

She spun around with a warm look in her eyes. "It's Maeve."

Ernest responded with another friendly nod. As he waited for her, he sunk deep into thought, observing everything around him. He marveled at the enormous stone inn with its original wooden beams. The large hearth at the far end was glowing bright, crackling and popping loudly as if trying to join in the guests' conversations. It was all so warm and inviting, he had to find Wilbur and bring him here. He pictured him curled up in front of the blazing fire, and his yearning only grew stronger. There had to be a good place to start. Should he go back to the scene of the crash? Would Wilbur have thought to return there and wait? Or did he just keep running? The latter thought made a pit in his stomach. He traced his shaking finger along the drawing in front of him.

Soon, Maeve returned with tea, scones, and bacon rolls. Everything smelled wonderful, but his stomach felt like a huge knotted ball. He tried his best to take a few bites, if only for the sake of being polite. He and Maeve sat opposite each other on the old wooden stools, sipping their tea in silent thought. The medieval inn groaned in the wind as if it was trying to deliberate right along with them.

CHAPTER FOUR

Wilbur awoke with his fur sparkling in the sun. The morning dew clinging to each and every one of his fine hairs. He noticed right away that it had stopped raining, and he was grateful. Though the friendly tree did indeed help to keep him dry. He also quickly realized that his paw wasn't hurting anymore. The glass must have

finally pushed its way out during the night. Well this was a good start, he thought. He slowly stood, and stretched himself out. His stomach grumbled loudly. He shook himself off, and decided he'd allow himself to find some food and water, but only quickly. Then, he would find Ernest.

He was convinced that today would be the day. Now that the storm had cleared, Wilbur's senses seemed once again to be in full working order. Nose to the ground, he set off deeper into the forest and didn't look back. There were so many smells. His senses really had come back, and everything was more intense than ever. As the long grass tickled his nose he smelled the musky scent of a male deer who must have passed through just a few hours before. Then, the fleeting scent of a female squirrel trailed by her young. He was tempted to follow their path, but he shuttered at the thought of eating tiny baby squirrels.

The unmistakeable smell of humans dashed in and out of his nose. That was curious. Why here? He thought about trying to find them, but just as quickly a new scent flew into his nose... this one was good. Fish, not far away. Wilbur picked up the pace to a trot, heading straight for a large river. As he reached the bank, it was quickly apparent that the water was ice cold, but it was soothing on his warm tired paws. He waited like a statue for an unsuspecting fish to swim by. Not even a hair on his ear twitched. The fog swirled around him and came in thicker than before. His nose almost burned with the intensity of this strange environment. He'd never experienced anything like it. He remained still.

After a very long time, Wilbur started to lose his patience. Ernest was more urgent, and he felt he was wasting time. Maybe he should just forget eating. His stomach growled in protest. He stood firm, and sniffed the air for any other options. His ear tilted toward a soft rippling in the water, finally a rainbow trout began to mosy through unawares. Its iridescent scales shimmering beneath the clear water. Wilbur shook with anticipation and tried to steady himself. As the trout turned his wide eyes toward his predator, it was too late. A giant splash and he was in Wilbur's teeth. Wilbur walked back up the bank with pride. As he began to tear into his well-caught meal, a rabbit wearily approached. Wilbur eyed him curiously, but continued to eat.

"Ahem."

Wilbur side-eyed the rabbit, surely that noise didn't just come from it... He looked around confused.

"Ahem... Hi... Over here." The softest and tiniest voice made its way through the fog.

Wilbur was shocked... how could it speak? He couldn't understand. The river's calming babble became louder. The fog seemed to whisper to him. Never in his life had he heard anything but the humans speak. What was this place he had come to? He swallowed hard, forgetting he had this fish in his mouth. He couldn't take his eyes off the little creature. He found himself hoping he'd speak again. As he watched him intently, he noticed that he had a large scar on his chest that parted his tawny brown fur. Instantly Wilbur took pity on him. "I wonder how that happened." Wilbur thought, but the rabbit looked at him as if he had spoke aloud. Wilbur quickly closed his mouth. He looked at the rabbit for a reaction. "Did I just?" He thought, or spoke, again. This time he heard his own voice. He was incredibly concerned now, and a bit embarrassed. His voice was strangely calming like a windy Summer's day. His jaw was left agape as the fish rolled away from his paws. The rabbit giggled. Wilbur was baffled.

"Oh don't mind that old scar...I had an encounter with a badger. They can be so cross sometimes. Is it okay if I sit with you? I don't need any of your food." He inched slightly closer. His voice was so soft and squeaky. Wilbur studied him some more. He looked at the small rabbit thoughtfully and nodded, still in shock that they were speaking to each other... that *he* was speaking. Maybe it was a dream? Was this all a dream? Could he wake up and Ernest would be there? He closed his eyes tightly. After a few seconds, Wilbur opened his eyes again and looked down to find the strange and happy little creature staring at him.

Not a dream. The little voice came again. "What's the matter? Didn't know you could talk huh? Happens a lot with the new ones." The rabbit was genuine, he scooted even closer. Wilbur tilted his head as he contemplated. He never thought he could and he certainly never tried it. New ones? What did this little creature mean by new ones? The rabbit just smiled at him and nestled into his haunch. Wilbur looked down at him again, utterly perplexed. He pulled the half-eaten fish back over with his teeth and tossed the rabbit a small piece. He shyly took it. They ate quietly together. Wilbur wasn't sure what he was afraid of, but the fear was there and he wasn't entirely sure what to do.

After long moments of silence, Wilbur was desperate. He took a deep breath and tried his hardest to form something... words? thoughts?

"Have you seen a tall human around these woods? He would be wearing wool trousers and a hat. One of the ones that go flat at the front." Wilbur was still shocked at how easy it was to speak. Had he always been able to do this? Could he talk to Ernest? The thought made him excited. He looked down at the rabbit hopefully.

"You'll get used to it, speaking I mean." He smiled, "And I don't believe I've seen your friend, I'm sorry. Probably a good thing though, if he's your friend. You wouldn't want to see him here. My name is Pippin by the way, what's yours?" He gave a small bounce of excitement.

"It's Wilbur, but what do you mean? Why wouldn't I want to see him here? I love him. He's my best friend, and I must find him. The sooner the better." Wilbur's eyes began to glaze over.

"Oh, no reason. Just kind of a scary forest to get lost in. Much better off finding him somewhere nice I would think... um do you know where you are?" The little rabbit struggled to hide his concern.

Wilbur shook his head. "Only that it's some sort of forest. I've never seen anything like it, I must admit."

Pippin was silent, Wilbur felt a little paw rest comfortingly on his leg. The tiny creature rubbed the tip of his long brown ear. They looked out into the distance for a while. As Wilbur started to settle into the somewhat concerning silence, Pippin suddenly stood up.

"Well I guess that's enough silence and thinking for one day huh Willy? That's what I'm going to call you from now on I think. Anyways... I was wonderin... Would you like me to help you look for your friend? It's dangerous for me alone out here and I've never really had many friends. You could be my trusty steed and I shall be your noble guide! I know these woods like the back of my lucky foot. You can count on me." Pippin puffed out his tiny chest.

Wilbur was about to say no, but the poor thing looked so intent on the idea. He couldn't refuse him. It couldn't hurt to have an extra pair of eyes he supposed. "Thank you Pippin, I think having an extra set of eyes is a good way to go." Wilbur attempted a soft awkward smile. He could only hope he was doing this talking thing correctly. He took a long stretch.

"Great! We'll just need to make a quick pit stop at home. I'll need to grab us some food, a map, binoculars, blankets, my rucksack..."

"Hold on a second... I'm afraid I've already been gone much too long... Ernest is probably scared out of his wits. We've never been apart... and he won't be able to go to work alone.. He needs me." He said worriedly.

"Oh come on Willy, we have to be proper adventurers if we are going to find a human in this ginormous forest!" His tiny arms stretched as wide as they could.

"Well alright... but please, let's try and be quick." Wilbur took a bow so that his rabbit friend could climb on. After much ado and a rabbit foot to the eye, they were off. Wilbur began to trot deeper into the wood, and Pippin shouted directions like a captain on a ship.

"You can call me Pip if you want. This is so great! Pip and Willy! Willy and Pip!" he squeaked. Wilbur glanced back at the way he'd come and let out a slightly concerned sigh, but he carried on.

SHORTLY, THEY ARRIVED AT A LARGE OAK TREE with a small red door cut into the trunk. Two round windows hung at either side. There was a small garden to the right and a quaint mailbox made out of what appeared to be a hollowed-out acorn. Wilbur marveled at how miniature everything was. He'd never seen anything like this. What was this place? He took another bow to let Pippin slide down. His rabbit friend waddled over to the house, pulled open the tiny door, and shortly disappeared up the winding stairs.

Wilbur definitely could not fit inside, but he was rather curious. He approached the small door and stuck his head in as far as it would go. There was a living area complete with a very small fireplace, a kitchen with a table and chairs made out of large mushrooms, and even a bathroom with a small tub, which looked to be made from a broken jam jar. Wilbur took in all the sights and smells as he excitedly looked around. He was careful not to let his nose knock anything over. He decided he would definitely have to bring Ernest back here to see this. As he slowly turned his head for one more look, his snout bumped into something.

"Hello!" A small voice giggled. Shocked, Wilbur looked cross-eyed at the rabbit standing on the end of his nose. She was even smaller than Pippin and wore a purple flower in one ear. "What's your name?" She asked politely.

"Oh, um hello there! My name is Wilbur. Sorry for the intrusion." He said as he pulled his head slowly out of the little red door.

"It's very nice to meet you, my name is Violet!" She said sweetly. As she hopped out the door, Wilbur noticed she had almost the same scar as Pippin. It struck diagonally across her chest, her sandy blonde fur almost bare where it touched.

"Nice to meet you as well, I am just waiting for..."

"Me!" Squealed Pippin as he came down the stairs, carrying what seemed to be an entire house full of things. Wilbur noticed a map, a captain's hat, a picnic basket, a large blanket, and a rubber duck, and he couldn't quite make out the rest. Pippin reached the bottom of the stairs and dropped everything onto the floor in a large heap. "He's waiting for me..." Pippin continued out of breath.

"Where are you guys going with all this stuff?" Violet pried.

"Wilbur and I are going on a perilous journey to find his friend Ernest. Through mountains uncharted, forests unnamed, and rivers untouched! And it's too dangerous for little sisters." He shot Violet a look. Wilbur fought back another worried sigh, it came slowly through his nose.

"I need to find my best friend. We shouldn't be away too long. I'm sure he's around here somewhere." Wilbur gave Violet a thoughtful smile. He felt bad that she'd have to stay by herself in the tree. She seemed so young.

"I never get to go on adventures. You never take me, Pippin..." She crossed her arms and huffed.

"You know why, it's too dangerous out there. You're better off here where the neighbors can keep an eye on you. I don't want you getting hurt again." Pippin seemed to soften.

"Fine... I'll keep watch over the fort! I guess I could raise the flag for your return." Violet scurried up to a string hanging near the window. She pulled and pulled until a large flag was hoisted and waved in the wind. It resembled a Jolly Roger but with a rabbit's skull in place of a human's and adorned with cross-bone carrots. She stood there looking up, seeming very proud of her work. Wilbur sat down and appreciated it as well. He gave Violet another smile. What a strange place, he thought.

"Thank you." He told her, gently. Violet beamed and hopped back over to the door. Pippin had grabbed a large rucksack and was filling it with all of his "adventure gear. He pulled out a small tan waistcoat and proudly fastened it on. In its little pocket, he placed a very tiny pocket watch. Wilbur watched him intently.

"Wilbur, where did you last see your friend?" Violet piped up.

"Well, I fear it was a long way outside of the forest. We spun out of control when the weather got bad. Ernest is a hearse driver you see, he takes people who have passed away to their final place and buries them. I do believe it's the greatest of all the human work. I would tell him that, but I never knew how, well maybe I might now? Either way, I always go to work with him... I always have until now. We were working when it happened. The windows shattered and I panicked and started running, which I am rather embarrased about I have to say... and that's when I lost him and ended up here. He could be anywhere by now." As Wilbur said those words he felt his hopefulness flicker like a candle.

"How awful. Please don't feel bad Wilbur, Ernest will understand. I know he will! I really hope you and Pippin find him. I'll keep my eyes out for him too, but hopefully he's not here." Violet said thoughtfully.

Wilbur looked at her, concerned. "Why would it be so bad to find him in here?" He saw Pippin shoot his sister another glance.

"This forest is just very big and scary, everyone here gets lost pretty easily. I hope he made it to a village. It would be easier for you to find him there I think. That's all." Violet explained throwing a small look back to her brother. She smiled and then ran over to hug Wilbur's leg. "I believe in you Wilbur, you'll find your friend." Wilbur smiled to thank her again for her kindness. She stood at the door and placed a small paw over her head giving them a salute.

"Well, are we finally ready Pippin?"

"We are fit to be the finest adventurers in the land Willy!" He straightened his coat and placed his captain's hat on. Wilbur noticed him take a dignified peek at his pocket watch. "Best be off now. We're burning daylight!" Pippin turned and saluted his sister back. Wilbur smiled and tried his best to do the same as he bowed down one more time for his little friend to climb aboard. They turned and swiftly headed off down a new trail behind the rabbits' cozy home.

"Where to Captain Pippin? We have no time to lose." Wilbur tried his best to glance back. Pippin stood and pointed straight out into the distance holding onto his hat. He looked very proud to be addressed as *Captain*.

"We head North. I have an idea of someone who may be aware of Ernest's whereabouts. He sees everything in this forest, despite his...impairments."

Wilbur was nervous, but intrigued. They started into a steady jog. A warm inviting breeze blew through their fur.

CHAPTER FIVE

"Oh! I almost forgot we have to get down to the print shop before Uncle Ben closes up."

Her voice aroused Ernest from his thoughts, and he watched as Maeve hurriedly tidied up around the inn. Frantically, she raced over towards the giant medieval door and grabbed a long camel-colored coat and hat off of a hook. "Thomas!" She sang out as she fiddled with her many buttons. A short man with red hair appeared from within the small kitchen. "Please look after the place for a bit while Ernest and I go down to Uncle Ben's. Shouldn't be too busy for you. Bar and kitchen close in a few hours anyway." Thomas nodded warmly as Maeve tossed him a ring of keys.

Ernest hurried to his feet and tugged on his flat cap, gently placing his tea cups and plates to the side. Maeve spun on a heel to face him. "Well let's go slow poke! We've got a best friend to find don't we?" She smiled at him as if fishing for some positivity, and against his will, Ernest felt his cheeks go red. He just as quickly shook it off, and they were out the door.

They walked swiftly through the sleepy old town, and their heels echoed on the ancient cobblestone streets. The smell of bread was wafting away in the distance as the evening started to creep in. Many of the townsfolk stepped out of their cozy stone homes. They struggled into their rain coats and wellies begrudgingly leaving their warm fires, as they set off to give their dogs their final walk of the day. Ernest looked down at his feet.

"You'll find Wilbur." Maeve gave him a squeeze on the shoulder.

He returned her words with a small smile. "Maeve... I meant to ask you. Genuinely, how did you get Wilbur's likeness so spot on?"

She hesitated for a minute as his question hung in the chilly spring air. "Well... sometimes I have dreams. Not just any dreams. They're often very vivid, and these certain dreams usually end up being some sort of a vision or premonition. I don't know it seems a bit silly doesn't it?" She paused and Ernest could tell she felt embarrassed, he did his best to give her a reassuring glance. "... It's been this way since I was a little girl, and last night after you came in asking around for Wilbur, I dreamt about him. He was running around what looked like a yew tree and I was watching him. Then, he ran into a strange forest and I woke up. I do apologize for not being more open about it. I don't like to mention my dreams much. You know how people can get." She nervously fingered the hem of her coat. Her sheepish breath betrayed by the nippy air like the white puffs from a steam engine.

Ernest studied her and nodded thoughtfully. He walked silently for a few beats. He wanted her to know that this was a safe place. Who was he judge? "The yew tree... that's peculiar. I don't think I ever mentioned how I lost Wilbur in the first place." He eyed Maeve biting her lip, he was waiting for her to take the bait and she for him to continue. He obliged. "I was so frantic I must've skipped over the whole story. That night, we were delivering a man to his resting place, Wilbur and I. He was a soldier, another who passed in Germany. Very young and handsome, and it never gets easier to see these things, I'm an undertaker you see..." His voice trailed off and he felt himself nervously waiting for a reaction.

The mention of his occupation often got mixed signals, but one look to Maeve and her patient smile told him everything. A small sigh of relief escaped him. "Anyway, as we were coming out of a petrol station the fog started to roll in something fierce. I looked over at Wilbur and the next thing I knew we were violently skidding off the road. I eventually came to in the hearse and there was glass everywhere. We were crumpled front end first into a very large yew tree... and Wilbur was gone." They both walked on in silence, trying to grasp for any words that would help in some way.

Maeve gently placed a hand on his shoulder again. "I'm so sorry Ernest. That must have been truly awful for the both of you. You're certainly lucky to be alive... Poor Wilbur must be terrified out there." She paused. "Is it worth checking the forest? The one in my dream, near the yew?" She asked softly.

"I did, right after I came to. No sign of him. Though the fog was still very thick now that it's coming back to me. It would probably be worth another look." He felt his face crease deeply into worry.

"Strange isn't it? The fog there seems to hang around most days. It isn't the first time that forest has popped up in my dreams. I have yet to figure it out, but it gives me the creeps." She trembled and shook her head. "Listen, how about we get these posters done, and then maybe tomorrow we can have another look around the area? Maybe we will have better luck with four pairs of eyes."

Ernest gave a half-hearted smile and nodded. Just as he was about to thank her again, Maeve sharply turned left and swiftly headed for a large door. As Ernest caught up, she was already giving it a good knock. Ernest looked up and read the green and gold sign. *Ben's Prints and Things*

"Uncle Ben! I know you're still here. I see the lights on!" Maeve called out while jiggling the gold door handle. A small black cat gracefully jumped into the window. He climbed atop a large stack of papers and shimmied himself between some falling signs. Ernest couldn't help but be intrigued. "Hello Pendle, where on Earth is your father?" Maeve asked the strange cat, who looked very unimpressed. Just then, a man's voice came muffled from the other side.

"Just a minute Maeve! Jiminy Crickets!" The door swung open and a befuddled old man in a white button-up, tweed pants, and black suspenders stood at the other side. He had a shuffled stack of papers in one hand and a cup of tea in the other. He slowly reached up with his wrist to try and adjust his large round glasses. Ernest noticed he had spilled tea on his white mustache and it had trickled down his shirt. He seemed very confused.

"I am so sorry Uncle Ben, we needed to use your mimeograph before you closed up shop." She smiled sheepishly.

"You need what?! Bloody hell Maevey, I was just tidying up and making a brew. I wasn't goin anywhere. I thought you'd seen a murder, the way you was pounding!" He put down his papers and smoothed back what was left of his snow-white hair. He took a step back and motioned them inside. "Come come, sorry about the mess here, uh what was your name son?"

"Ernest sir, thank you for letting us in I apologize for such short notice..." He shot Maeve a look. She promptly shrugged it off.

"This is Ernest and he has recently lost his dog, Wilbur, so I need to make a wax stencil of this drawing I did and quickly." She held it up to her uncle's face. "I figured we could make lost dog posters. I thought it was a pretty good idea myself, but as I said this is really quite urgent and you're the only one with a mimeograph and also standing in my way. You two should get on marvelously." She waved her hand in a half motion that was meant to be an introduction and then hurried around the corner.

Ben sat down on a chair nearby, rubbed his face, and laughed. "Maevey is a bit of a character she is." He said smiling. Ernest smiled too and nodded in agreement. He took a seat on a small wooden chair nearby, taking in all the machinery that crowded the shop. "She has a heart of gold though, my Maevey. That's for sure." Ben sipped what was left of his tea and fussed with the stain on his shirt.

"Yes sir, I barely know her, but those two things I found out very quickly. It's incredibly nice of her to help me as much as she is." Ernest continued to look around curiously.

"Aye, she has some special things about her. She's more like a daughter to me to tell you the truth, her mum passed many moons ago and her dad runs a freight business down south. The fool is never around. He sort of just threw the inn at Maeve a few years ago and she's taken it in stride, and it's the best damn inn for miles around!" He said loud enough for her to hear. "Bless her..." He added softly. Ernest marveled at the man's interesting demeanor and what he picked out to be a very Somerset-sounding accent, which he always found very comforting. He turned his gaze gently toward the corner where he could hear Maeve stenciling away.

"I must say this is a really interesting place you have here. It's the most comprehensive amount of printing equipment I have ever seen. When did you establish yourself? If you don't mind me asking."

"Ah thank you, my boy, the passion has sort of consumed me. Especially after the passing of my lovely Alice. Let's see um... she left us in 1930, and I opened up here about 5 years after that. So since 1935. Ten years of printing everything you could imagine." The old man beamed behind his large spectacles.

Ernest could tell he was very proud. "You have done a lovely job, and I couldn't be more grateful for you letting us use your instruments, and I'm sorry to hear about your Alice as well." He mustered a gentle smile. Ben gave an appreciative nod as he sipped the last of his tea. Pendle jumped off of his paper stack and purred his way over to Ernest. "Have you been rather busy with the war going on then?"

"Aye... think I could ask the same of you." Ben replied, eyeing the dirt stains along Ernest's pants and jacket. Ernest felt oddly exposed and tried to cross his legs. How did he know Ernest was an undertaker? Just from the dirt stains? He kept quiet as Ben continued. "Yeah not too bad for us print shops I'd say. Shame really. Never feels good to profit from such devastation. Though someone has to do it I spose... Ah, I see you've met my useless cat. Never caught a mouse in his life. He's rather good at finding things I've lost though, I'll give him that." Ernest chuckled and began to scratch Pendle under his chin. Ben stood up from his chair, shook his head lovingly, and sighed. "Well, cup of tea then Ernest?"

"That would be nice, thank you."

"Ah that a boy, won't be a moment." He stiffly made his way up the stairs. Ernest stood and walked around the corner to peek in on Maeve and the magical mimeograph. Pendle was right on his heels.

The mimeograph was happy with Maeve's newly etched wax stencil. She slowly inserted the stencil, lined up a full paper ream, and poured a large bottle of black ink into the port at the top. As she pulled the crank at the side, the mimeograph roared to life. Inking, stamping, and rolling. Ernest stood behind and watched in awe. A perfect drawing of Wilbur appeared over and over again. Finally, Maeve gently pulled the long line of paper out of the machine. She grabbed a pair of scissors and handed another pair to Ernest. They sat down at a large oak table and started carefully cutting out each poster, separating it from the next. Ben cautiously came down with a full plate of biscuits and three cups of tea.

He turned an old oil lamp on and sat down on the floor amongst the flood of paper.

They each hand-wrote Wilbur's name and the address of the inn on every poster, followed by the word **LOST** in big letters. Tears began to form in Ernest's eyes. He hurriedly wiped them away and gave his new friends a thankful smile. Pendle jumped onto the table and walked across every single poster with an inky foot. Maeve couldn't contain herself and started to giggle. Ernest and Ben joined in with full-bellied laughter. The laughs continued as they slowly tidied up the shop.

"Well, we must be going Uncle Ben. Thank you so much for lending the mimeograph and for those lovely biscuits!" Maeve smiled and gingerly gathered all of the posters. "And thank *you* Mr. Pendle for your fine signature," she added playfully. Ernest smiled and reached out to shake Ben's hand.

"No problem at all my dear, mind those posters. They may be a bit wet yet." He announced as he began to wipe up the ink stains along the table.

Ernest helped gather their coats and hats as they shuffled towards the door. "Thank you kindly, sir, I'm sure we'll be back with an update for you. Hopefully a positive one at that!"

"Ah please do keep me in mind. I really hope you find your friend Wilbur. If I or Pendle can be of any more assistance please let us know." He threw the inky rag over his shoulder and approached the door to show them out, with Pendle close behind.

"We will sir, you did say Pendle here was good for finding things." Ernest looked down at the mysterious little cat.

"We may borrow him from you Uncle Ben..." Maeve joked as she bent down to give Pendle a scratch. Ben chuckled and politely waved them off. Pendle gave them a little wink and a flick of his tail. Ernest and Maeve exchanged curious glances as they made their way down the dusky streets. Guided by the warm street lamps and a friendly nod from the man in the moon, they headed back to the inn. Ernest was starting to feel a bit more hopeful.

Chapter Six

As they walked through the sun-dappled trees, Wilbur could hear water close by. Sure enough, they soon came upon another large river, but this one was moving at a frightening pace. Wilbur skidded to a halt as the water swirled and roared.

"What's the matter, Wilbur?" Pippin asked excitedly.

Wilbur looked up trying to see the little bunny on his back. "Are you seeing what's in front of us Pip? I'm not so sure I can swim through that…"

"Sure you can! I've waded this river many times. A few years ago Violet and I made waxcap boats and raced them here. We got through unharmed...mostly." The little rabbit exclaimed confidently.

Wilbur felt his hackles raise at the "mostly" part. He felt Pippin wasn't telling the whole truth, but he did admire his courage. "I don't know Pippin... this looks treacherous to me. What happens if we... don't make it?...I'll never find Ernest." Wilbur stared down at the tumultuous water lapping his paws. His heart beat quickened.

"Nonsense, that's basically impossible! Nothing is too big, nothing is too fearsome for Captain Pippin and his trusted friend and steed! Think of Ernest, and go forth my brother."

Wilbur could feel Pippin take a steady bracing stance, his fur was taught as Pippin grabbed on with all of his tiny might. Wilbur couldn't help but let a nervous smile escape. He slowly stepped deeper into the chilling water. In an instant, the water had risen to his shoulders. Pippin's little paws now became a death grip on his neck. The water splashed and spat at Wilbur's face in icy waves. They were carried this way and that, and he tried his best to swim straight on. For the first time, Pippin wasn't shouting any captain's orders. It was obvious neither of them felt very confident anymore. The water was angry.

Wilbur trembled, but he kept the image of Ernest firmly in his mind. He paddled forward as hard as he could. The water spray was a constant cloud on his vision, but through the droplets he could see that they were almost at the bank on the other side. His paws began to touch the gravel again. Relief washed over him as Pippin started to loosen his grip, but then the tiny weight on his back started to slide. He couldn't see over his shoulder, but he could only hope Pippin was holding out. He gave one last push to get them onto sturdy ground, but the weight on his back had gone completely.

Wilbur clambered onto the bank and spun around. His eyes frantically searched the rushing water. Then, just off shore he spotted Pippin's long ears on the surface, only about a meter away. But the tiny rabbit was floating and still. Wilbur had no time to panic, he jumped back into the bone-chilling water without a thought. He could see Pippin's ears moving rapidly downriver. Wilbur swam hard and fast. A large log came racing downstream and missed his head by a few centimeters. His breath was getting shallow and hard to catch. Pippin was just out of reach. One last stretch of his neck and his teeth finally made contact with the tiny tweed jacket. Wilbur raised his head out of the water as much as possible, trying to keep Pippin well out of the spray. He spluttered and struggled until they finally reached the rocky bank once more.

Wilbur found his footing and bounded up the bank with one last burst of energy. He carefully laid his friend down on a nearby patch of moss. Pippin was still unresponsive. Wilbur began to lick him desperately. His little rabbit feet were cold and wet. Wilbur started to whimper. "Please don't leave me little friend... I can't lose another one." Wilbur collapsed in a heap of exhaustion as his chest heaved with sadness. Somberly, he laid his nose on Pippin's soft stomach. Time passed slowly. His eyes fluttered open and closed as he fought to stay awake. "Please Pippin...come back" He whispered, his eyes coming to a close. "This can't be the end... It can't." His words were heavy and barely made a sound.

Wilbur's eyes sprung open. He stood up quickly. Pippin began to twitch and groan. "Pippin! Are you there? Are you alright?! Please be alright..."

"Wilbur?" Pippin slowly opened his eyes and tried to get himself into a sit.

"Oh, Pippin! Oh, thank goodness you're okay. Please take it slowly." Wilbur bent down to nudge his friend up against a rock for support.

Pippin looked confused as he started to squeeze the water from his ears. "I'm sorry I fell off, I was just so cold and I couldn't feel my paws anymore...Oh no... My hat..."

Wilbur just shook his head in dismay. "That's what you're worried about?!"

Pippin looked down, slightly ashamed. Wilbur looked at him sitting there soaked and sad. He knew the little thing was really trying. Wilbur gave a half-hearted chuff and trotted down to the water's edge. He spotted the hat and backpack tangled in some reeds. He gathered them gently in his teeth and returned to his friend. The fragile little bunny beamed, and light returned to his big brown eyes. Wilbur smiled. "Much obliged, Captain Pip... but try not to abandon your ship next time." He sat down on the bank with his tiny friend who only nodded at him shyly. For a long while they sat in silence and and let the warm sun dry their fur.

"You're my best friend..." Pippin said suddenly and softly, gently touching Wilbur's snout.

"Alright alright... don't we have somewhere to be?" Wilbur said with a loving look.

"Right! Yes, onward once again!" He fastened his soggy hat and ascended onto Wilbur's back.

A small groan escaped from Wilbur as he stretched in preparation for another long journey. His heart was heavy and cumbersome, but maybe just a little bit less so now. "We're coming Ernest." He said, as his paws began to thud against the ancient forest floor once again.

CHAPTER SEVEN

Pendle waited for his master to take his evening nap, before slyly slipping out of the print shop door. Blending seamlessly into the shadows and dark alleyways, his paws silently pittered along the cobblestones. He had to find that yew tree, and Wilbur. Through countless dreams and overheard conversations, he knew more than enough. He had to tell Wilbur everything. Within the very short time he'd known the man in the flat cap, he grew quite fond of him. He knew he was pure of heart and pure of soul, a rare trait within the humankind. He had a feeling Wilbur would be the same. Though he didn't normally fancy dogs, he figured this was an exception. For a terrible wrong always had to be made right. Ernest and Wilbur must know, they must find each other. One way or another.

CHAPTER EIGHT

Wilbur's paws had started to ache. He swore Pippin had told him they were almost there an hour ago. He'd given his captain's orders of "Just follow this path until you see The Valley of the Pines" and then promptly fell asleep. It felt as if they had been walking for days. Wilbur was now concerned that he'd somehow missed a plethora of pine trees. He opened his mouth to wake Pippin, when a strong scent smacked him in the nose. It was the strongest scent of pine and cedar wood he had ever smelled. He kept his nose right to the ground. Pippin began wriggling around.

"Oh good, you found it!" Pippin said with a yawn.

"Thanks for the help…" Wilbur rolled his eyes. His ears twitched back as he heard Pippin wrestling with his map.

"The Old Pines should be right up ahead according to my maps. Wilbur, remember we have to be silent when we approach. Rell doesn't like loud noises. His hearing is quite possibly the best in the world."

As they neared the ancient pine trees, Wilbur heard what he thought was a strange wind blowing through. Quickly, he realized it was no wind at all. It was the ghost-like wing beats of something very large. Pippin climbed down and Wilbur came to a sit in complete silence. They waited. Wilbur's hairs stood on end. He was afraid to move. An enormous great-horned owl flew overhead. He circled back a few times, and it felt like an eternity until he finally floated silently down in front of them. Wilbur heard a pine needle fall and hit the dirt below. He studied the grand creature in front of them. His feathers were full and the color of dusty gold. His face was soft but strong and worn with what seemed to be centuries of wisdom. On final inspection, he noted the creature was missing an eye. Wilbur tried hard not to let his gaze linger. He felt Pippin inch closer to his flank.

"And what brings you to the pines my good fellows?"

The creature's voice rang out, it sounded as if he were an ancient god of the druids. An avalanche that steadily tumbled down the mountainside. Wilbur remembered to speak quietly. The words fell clumsily into the air.

"Hello Sir Rell... my name is Wilbur and this is my friend Pippin. Our request is a simple one and hopefully won't trouble you too much. We are aware that you know most if not everything that happens in this forest." The old owl shifted and seemed to sit up a bit more pridefully. "Well Sir, I've lost my best friend Ernest. This was only a couple of days ago... I need to find him, Sir. I've had no luck on my own. I've been wandering here for what seems like ages and still nothing. If it helps, I can tell you he's tall and wears a cap. His trousers are held up by straps. He is really so kind-hearted, and gentle... and.." Wilbur felt his voice shake.

"Ahhh... so we have another lost soul. There are many of you here. Many of you seeking your way through this forest. However, I'm sorry to tell you sweet Wilbur, but I have not seen your friend. Perhaps he has been through already? I can only offer a small bit of guidance. For there is one place you may find him yet." His celestial eye focused, unblinking, on Wilbur.

"Yes, please Sir... anything you can tell us. Anything at all." Wilbur felt Pippin gently stroking his side. He had remained very quiet.

"Indeed I will share with you what I know to be true. There is a willow tree at the center of this wood. Around its base grow many flowers of every color. The journey is quite long, but many who are lost gather there. The ones who are looking for something. If your friend is looking for you as well, as you believe him to be, then he may be waiting there. There is a fox who lives near the willow. He can help you if you have further questions. He knows things beyond our realm of understanding." The ancient thing took a pause to breathe, he closed his one eye for a moment. "This forest is very large Wilbur, it holds many secrets and many of these creatures will never find their way out. Sadly, it has been this way for many centuries. This journey you're on is one of the spirit as much as it is of the body. You will be tested, and you must remain strong. Offer help when you can, and it will not go unnoticed." His voice echoed along the trees for so long that it seemed the trees began talking to each other.

Wilbur wasn't sure what to make of everything. Why are there so many lost here? Would that make it harder to find Ernest? Who would need his help? He gave himself a small shake to try and clear his head. Subconsciously, he bowed to the owl in thanks. He spoke nervously. "Thank you, Sir Rell, you have no idea how grateful I am. I will take your advice as best I can. Here, please take some of our food as a gift for your generous help." He gently tipped Pippin's tiny rucksack with his nose to look for some rations, but the great owl was already lifting his wings. The wind swirled around them, warm and sweetly scented.

"Nonsense, I need only for you to listen and to heed what I've said. Remember dear Wilbur, sometimes the most potent truths are not the ones spoken by ancient gods, but the ones that are hiding in our hearts." The gigantic bird peered down at Pippin from the sky, and took his leave. As the wind settled there was only silence and sunset. Wilbur watched the great owl make his exit soaring higher still into the dusky sky. The nerves gave way to an excitement that began to burn through him like a wildfire. Rell's final words had barely made it through to him. He tapped his paws with anticipation and looked down at Pippin who looked smaller than ever.

"He's gone now Pip, you don't need to be frightened. I'm here with you." He said reassuringly. Pippin shyly nodded his head. "We need to find this willow tree. Ernest will be there. I know he will. I bet we can make it there in a day. I'll push myself as best as I can. I can't believe we may have found our answer. I was beginning to think this was some sort of awful nightmare, but this could really be it! Right, come on then. All aboard Captain Pip, I believe in you!" Wilbur gave a smile and bent down quickly, tail wagging. Pippin looked down at the ground for a moment, he climbed on, nervously crumpling his captain's hat in his paws. They started into a run, and Pippin quietly held on.

CHAPTER NINE

Ernest walked slowly down a narrow lane and listened to the light rain all around him. As he reached the end of the lane, there was a small haberdashery. He decided he'd hang the last remaining poster of Wilbur here. Carefully he unfurled the crisp new paper and nailed in each corner, just to the left of the doorway. He was sure to place all the posters near storefronts. He hoped they'd be more easily seen this way. Ernest sighed and took a small step back. The haberdashery was empty and quiet. He supposed everyone had gone home for a nice cozy evening. He stared longingly at the final drawing of his friend, whose eyes only stared lovingly back. He missed his own cozy evenings with Wilbur. His heart felt like a bag of mud, sticky and slow.

Gently, he placed his hand on the poster and murmured a small prayer that even he couldn't make much sense of. He just hoped it worked. It had been a few days now, and his hopes for finding Wilbur were dwindling by the minute. Why hadn't he come into the village? Surely he was clever enough to think that way. What if somebody had stolen him? Ernest shook his head trying to disperse the cloud of negative thoughts. He took a couple of deep breaths which quivered in the wind. Without thinking he whispered to the drawing of his best friend. "I better go and catch up with Maeve old buddy, please come back to me soon." Slowly he took his hand from the poster, and he noticed a man passing him by with a sorrowful smile.

A wave of self-consciousness washed over him, but he gave the man an almost grateful smile in return followed by a polite wave. Ernest turned and started walking in the direction of the inn. The rain started to subside and rays of sun poked through the desolate gloomy skies. Ernest stopped for a moment and looked around at the strange small town. He felt so at home ever since he had arrived. There was just something about it. The sun beams shun down brightly and warmed his skin. He knew Wilbur would be keen on it as well. He couldn't wait to show him all of the new places and smells.

On his way to the inn, Ernest decided to take the long way. He turned down the next street which ran parallel to the mysterious forest he'd searched before. As he walked, the buildings became much fewer and far between. He marveled at the large country homes, the many chimneys puffing out great plumes of warm cedar scented smoke. At the end of the road stood a large metal sign that read *Welcome to Asphodel On Eden.* He smiled to himself, realizing that he'd started to fall in love with a town he hadn't even known the name of. As he continued his stroll the smile kept his hope burning a little while longer, and he repeated the town's name a few times over. It really rolled off the tongue.

Without noticing he had come upon a large graveyard near the forest edge. "How do I always end up at a graveyard?" Ernest said half chuckling to himself. "Potential job I suppose. Maybe Wilbur and I could stay here, a nice change of scenery." He thought aloud. He headed towards the iron fence and looked over at the hundreds of old headstones. They dotted the deep green hills as far as the eye could see, their faint grey stone a melancholy contrast. It was a lovely property.

Death normally didn't bother Ernest, but in that moment he felt his eyes begin to well up. He was worried. That was the plain and simple truth, he was worried sick. It was the elephant in the room. Something he'd never say out loud. The worst scenario he could imagine. He wanted nothing more than to turn around and see Wilbur running into his arms... right now. He turned, with his breath held, eyes squinted, but there was only trees and the stone of a crumbling wall. He wiped his eyes, feeling a bit foolish. Of course it wasn't going to be that easy, but no matter how long it took he would never give up on his best friend, not in a million years.

A few rogue tears managed to make their way down, Ernest wiped his cheeks with his sleeves. He took a deep breath and left the old graveyard in his wake, making tracks for the inn once again. He watched the ominous outline of the forest as he walked. As he approached his final turn, he gave one more glance over his shoulder, and studied the mysterious forest that bordered Asphodel On Eden. But this time, there was a flash of black and white. He swore he saw it.

Ernest spun around and ran as fast as he possibly could. Within seconds he disappeared into the tree line, and within seconds he was surrounded by fog. An almost whisper like sound floated on the wind and barely tickled his ear.

"The Wil O The Whisp knows the way. The Wil O The Wisp... It knows Ernest."

Ernest shuttered and swatted at the voices like flies. He chalked it down to imagination. Though the voices didn't stop. Ernest stumbled through, his heart beating out of his chest, and his palms had broken into a cold sweat. Once again, the forest was impenetrable. He tried his hardest to make out anything at all. Touching his hands to the trees for balance, he called out.

"WILBUR! COME HERE, BOY! IT'S ERNEST!... WILBURRRR!" Ernest shouted as loud as he could, but he was muffled. The fog choked his words as soon as they escaped. The forest was unlike anything he'd ever seen. Endless, dark, and perpetually drowned in fog. It was somehow the loudest thing he'd ever experienced and the quietest. He could just make out the sun going down outside the forest, and he knew this place was dangerous, but he didn't care. He kept going, he had to. He'd never forgive himself if he didn't at least try. In the distance, the hazy outline of an enormous willow tree started to emerge. It looked as if it was perfectly centered. A strange glowing white figure was heading right for it. There was something very different to the first time Ernest had entered these woods. All of his hair stood on end. The shrieking voice came again.

"The Will O The Wisp is here. The Will O The Wisp will find Wilbur."

Ernest swatted at the nothingness. He covered his ears. "Please leave me alone! I'll find Wilbur on my own! I know what you are." He kept his hands tightly over his ears and waded towards the giant tree. As he got closer it seemed he was also getting further and further away. He ducked as a great horned owl swooped low over his head with a booming "Hooo."

"WILBURRRR! Please Wilbur...come back." His voice trailed off. He removed his flat cap and sobbed as he sat down on the cold Earth below. He tossed his hat into the dirt and placed his heavy head in his hands. "I don't know what to do boy... You've gotta find me. I can't be here. It won't let me." He said in soft desperation. Within a moment of his words, something brushed his leg... Ernest's head shot up and his body quickly followed. "Who's there?! Wilbur?!" He looked down as a small black cat brushed by him and quickly disappeared into the mist. "Pendle?! Hey... wait..." He tried his best to follow, but another voice crept through the silence. He braced himself to run.

"Ernest?!!! Are you here?!! Helloooo?"

Ernest was shocked to hear someone familiar... It was Maeve. "Maeve?! I am here!"

"I can barely hear you! Come towards my voice!" Her voice sounded as if she were miles away. Ernest gave one last look behind him, and hesitantly turned away from the willow tree. He walked back down the path he hoped he'd come from. As he neared the edge of the forest, the shrieking noises became more distant.

"I'm here Ernest! Follow my voice!" Her muffled shout came again.

"I'm coming Maeve. Keep talking and reach out your hands!" Ernest reached out as well.

"Over here!" She called.

He turned to the right and walked a few more paces. Trees, grass... hands. He clasped the hands tightly in his own and pulled. Maeve came bursting through the fog. She hugged him tightly.

"Ernest! I was worried sick... we said we'd come here together and look." She gave him a look of genuine concern.

"I know, I'm sorry. Let's get out of here and I'll explain." They walked hand in hand until they found the edge of the wood. As they stumbled out into the last light of dusk, Ernest knew exactly where they were. He looked over at the yew tree, standing gnarled and cracked where the hearse had hit. Its enormous bowing branches reached towards him. Reflections shun from flecks of glass that still hung onto the weeds. Maeve knowingly squeezed his hand. Ernest collapsed onto the ground, as the sadness overtook him again. Maeve quickly sat next to him and threw her arms around his shoulders.

"This is all my fault Maeve... where is my boy?!" He looked at her through drowning green eyes.

She hugged him tighter. "We will find him Ernest... soulmates don't lose each other forever." She smiled at him genuinely and sweetly.

Her smile was strangely so warm and familiar. It sparked the smallest ember of hope within him. Ernest wiped his face once again."I thought I saw him Maeve... I was walking back to the inn and I looked toward the forest... there was a flash of black and white. I know there was. So I just ran. I'm sorry, it was foolish." He felt a reassuring squeeze on his shoulder. "This bloody forest is impossible. I can't see even a foot in front of me. There's something in there as well Maeve something awful, and I'm worried that it took Wilbur. It tried to take me." He sniffled.

"The Wisp... I know." She looked down.

"The Wisp? As in a Will O The Wisp? I thought that's what it kept shrieking at me, but I didn't think those were real." Ernest's face went pale.

"Mhhmm, none of us did. I dream about the stupid thing all the time. Don't worry, it doesn't have an interest in animals."

"That somehow doesn't make me feel much better." Ernest said blankly.

"Sorry." Maeve let out a nervous laugh and shook her head. "They don't have much interest in animals. As long as you know not to follow it, you'll be okay. I can't really explain it but this town is strange Ernest, even more so this forest. Us townsfolk have just sort of come to terms with it I suppose." She gave him a friendly touch on the back. He couldn't really think of what to say. "I do believe that you saw him... I really do. I believe that he's in there somewhere, and we will find him. He's probably struggling to find his way out just as we are finding a way in...the poor thing. It's a god forsaken place this forest."

"So what do we do then?" Ernest asked, still unable to take his gaze from the distance.

"I've done a lot of research about this place. This forest has a strange tie to the ancient celts. It somehow correlates itself to the changing seasons."

"Don't all forests do that?" Ernest asked.

"Well yes, but I mean specifically this fog. Whenever there's an equinox it lifts. I'm really not sure why, but

I've proven it on every occasion. It's like a veil that lifts." She started to sound embarrassed.

"Maeve... I believe you. If this was a week ago I may have had a different response, but after what has just happened... I believe you." He was telling the truth. He paused to try and process his thoughts. "I'm almost relieved really that you've experienced all of these strange things as well. I thought I might've finally lost it." He felt as if he were in some sort of nightmare. He took a deep breath in and tried to steady his nerves.

"I know this is a lot. Just try and breathe. I'm glad you're with me so far. My thoughts were simply that we come back here on the Spring Equinox in a couple of days. We can bring some homemade treats for Wilbur to entice him. If the fog is lifted, like it usually is, then it'll be much easier for Wilbur to find us." She sounded hopeful. "A bit of an equinox picnic if you will."

"I'll try anything Maeve." Ernest replied, trying to turn his gaze back to her. She gave him another big squeeze of relief. A smile crept across his face.

"This is going to work Ernest! I can feel it."

He shyly reached over and touched her hand. "Thank you Maeve. For helping me with all of this." She smiled in return.

"Oh, I forgot to mention that I saw Pendle in there as well. I wanted to follow him, but then I heard you calling for me."

Maeve shot him a surprised look. "That's odd... he gets up to a lot of mischief that cat. I guess I shouldn't be so surprised. He probably has a second home in there." She giggled.

Ernest couldn't help but chuckle. "Yeah, he bumped my leg. Then just sort of disappeared." His brow lightly furrowed in thought.

"That is a bit strange I'll admit, but he does like a wander. He always has that smug little look on." She smiled to herself. "I bet you didn't know black cats are quite reknown for being messengers throughout folklore." A glint of mischief shun in her honey pot eyes.

"Are they?" He had to admit that was interesting. He'd never thought about cats much.

"Yeah, they're fantastic creatures. I'll lend you some books. Maybe he has a hunch... he does have a magical power." She smirked.

"Really? What could that possibly be?..." Ernest's eyes were wide as another smile started to force its way through.

Maeve leaned in close as if she were about to share a big secret. "Well he does this thing where he can always convince Uncle Ben to give him the last can of tuna. I think its a telepathic thing. Those enchanting green eyes of his." Maeve let herself give into her giggles.

Ernest just placed his hand over his face, she really had him going for a second. His nerves started to give way and the giggles bubbled up inside of him until they spilled over. It felt so nice to laugh, especially now. Wilbur never did like it when he was sad. He brushed his hair from his face and replaced his flat cap. He turned to Maeve again, "Do you think he could actually find Wilbur? Pendle I mean."

"Anything is possible, animals are incredible like that. Pendle has always been curious, and I think he can sense that something is wrong. He seemed to like you when we visited Uncle Ben. Maybe he can sense that you're not okay." She pulled up some grass and began to tie it in small knots.

"Yeah, I guess you're right… I'll take anybody's help right now." Ernest studied her movements.

She looked up at him suddenly. "Do you have an idea of Wilbur's favorite treats?" Her eyes beamed.

" I do have a list actually… He's a bit spoiled I suppose…" Ernest shook his head shyly. Maeve gave him a sweet look. They both laughed again. "You really are a wonderful person Maeve… I can't thank you enough. You never needed to help me, but you have in every single way. You've taken a chance on a complete stranger. Your heart is just so pure, and I'm truly grateful to have run into you in such a difficult time." Ernest smiled and took Maeve's warm soft hand in his own. He noticed her blush.

"You really don't have to thank me. I feel as if I've known you forever. I can't explain it… and it sounds daft… but I think we were meant to run into each other… and I will do whatever it takes to help you find your sweet little Wilbur. I'd hope somebody would do the same for me. I couldn't begin to imagine the pain you're in." Her eyes looked deeply into his, full of warmth and hope. "I desperately want to meet him as well. I'm sure he's just as lovely as you." She smiled and let her gaze drift to the warm pink horizon. Ernest reached out one hand and gently grasped both of hers. Her face curiously turned towards him, if only the slightest bit. She was glowing like some kind of sun faerie in the fiery golden sunset. He felt the nerves flooding throughout his entire body, but he wanted to take this chance. Maybe it was time he started really going for the things he wanted. He stared at her blushing cheeks, and her amber eyes so full of kindness, love, and what he was certain was a little hint of magic. Her heart-shaped lips slowly turned up into the lightest smile. He leaned in slowly, squeezed her hands, and kissed her cheek as daintily as a butterfly. His heart fluttered and he could tell hers did as well. Wilbur was going to absolutely adore her.

CHAPTER

TEN

Wilbur had run for almost a full day without a stop. His chest heaved. He slowed to a trot and then a walk. The big willow tree was farther than he expected. He didn't want to admit it, but he was tired. As much as his mind fought it, he figured they could do with a small rest. Pippin had remained eerily silent throughout their entire journey which had left Wilbur to navigate purely on instinct.

"Hey Pip, are you alright up there? You haven't said a word." His question was met only with more silence. Wilbur was concerned. "Pip... Are you ever going to speak again? I was thinking we could stop just for the smallest break, is that okay? We can maybe have a chat?" There was a long pause.

"Yeah that's okay. I'm alright… just tired I guess." His little voice sounded weary.

Wilbur felt him fiddle with the long hairs down the ridge of his back. They went on for a few minutes more until Wilbur stepped off into a small meadow of tall grass.

"This looks safe and comfortable. Only for a few minutes. Ernest will wait for me as long as he needs to, I know he will." He tried to mask the feelings of doubt that started to creep through him. Something wasn't sitting right. "We can't be too far off now, right Pip?"

Pippin slowly slid off Wilbur's back and made himself a bed between his big paws. More long moments of silence followed until finally he spoke. "Hey Wilbur, um how did you and Ernest meet?" He asked shyly.

Wilbur was surprised at the random question, but he liked this story so he obliged. Through his half-dreaming eyes, Wilbur began to float through his memories. "Well, I was born on a farm in the cold winter frost. I lived there a while with my mum and my siblings. It was really a lovely old place. There were so many animals, different ones at every turn. We were well taken care of. There was so much space to run and play and it was so green. Magnificent hills as far as the eye could see." He paused trying to hold onto the image. He felt Pippin snuggle in closer.

THE UNDERTAKER AND HIS DOG

"It was an amazing place to be a pup, I was lucky, until the day it all started to change. The farmers began taking us pups away one by one. They'd lead us out deep into the hills amongst the sheep. Day by day I would watch my brothers and sisters through the old wooden fence. They'd be gone for many hours and then finally they'd return entirely exhausted. Eventually, it was my turn. I learned that the farmers were training us to herd the sheep, and when it came to me, they were less than pleased. They would yell and scold me, and they became very cross. They said I was too playful. I never wanted to nip at the sheep, it felt mean and horrible, so I played with them instead. On cold nights I'd often snuggle up with them in the barn until I was told off. Sheep are lovely company really, and they became my friends. But the farmer's eventually lost their patience and decided I wasn't cut out for the job. I knew they wanted to send me away, and I was terrified. That's when Ernest showed up.

I walked out of the barn one sunny morning and he was standing there with his cap and the straps on his trousers. I peered out from behind the stone wall. The farmer pointed at me and Ernest knelt down with the kindest smile I've ever seen. I stood shyly in the corner and my tail gave into a little wag. My mother came from behind and nudged me towards him. She knew he was good. I gathered up what courage I had and bounded over to him. Before I knew what I was doing I had jumped all over his lap and kissed his face. He immediately returned the love and didn't mind the kisses. I'll never forget the smile he had that day. We needed each other. He scooped me up and loaded me into the hearse, and that was my life. To this day he has never scolded me, not once, and he likes to befriend the sheep as well. I miss him so much Pippin." Wilbur smiled as he drifted off. Pippin sniffled and stirred. He couldn't get to sleep.

"The Will O The Wisp Wilbur... it knows. Follow the Wisp..." Wilbur's ears twitched as he fought to try and stay asleep. The whispers went in and out of his ears and then they turned into shouts.

"Peter?!!! Peter?!"

Wilbur was quickly on his feet, accidentally knocking Pippin over. "Sorry, Pippin. Did you hear that?" He raised his upright ear a little higher.

"Hear what?" Pippin asked rubbing his eyes, half buried in the tall grass.

"Peter?!!" The voice came again.

"That! Come on. Maybe they've seen Ernest!" Wilbur gave a quick bow for his friend.

Pippin hurriedly climbed on and they started towards the voice. Wilbur finally found a woman standing now only a few meters away atop a large tree stump. She was clearly searching for something or someone. Immediately, she turned and noticed them. Her cheeks were faintly stained with tears. She was very kind looking with curly blonde hair. It was messily tied back and falling along her face. She wore a deep purple dress that had become tattered on the ends. She held a matching floral hat nervously in her hands.

"Oh! Hello there, what a curious sight." She let out a nervous chuff as she eyed captain-clad Pippin straddling Wilbur as best as he could. She pulled out her handkerchief and quickly wiped the tears from her face.

Wilbur went to greet her. "Whoof!" A sharp bark flew from him. He was confused… He tried once more to say hello. "Whoof!" A louder one this time. The woman gave a startled jump. Wilbur was anxious now, why couldn't he talk? He backed away and wagged his tail, trying to look more friendly. He desperately needed to ask the woman if she'd seen Ernest, and he wondered about Peter. Every time he tried to form the words, there was nothing but barks and whimpers. The woman seemed perplexed. She hesitantly held out a friendly hand. Wilbur approached slowly making sure he kept his tail wagging.

"Oh you poor dear, you seem worried. Are you looking for somebody as well? I've lost my son…Peter. He's only a little one. This place is awful. I can't seem to find my way anywhere." The sadness came over her again as she bent down to pet Wilbur.

Wilbur didn't know how to answer. He wanted to help her, to take her with to the old willow so she could find her son. He thought for a moment, and then quickly ran forward and dipped back over and over trying to tell her to follow. He ran back one more time with an excited bark and gave a soft nip on the hem of her dress.

She was startled, but she studied him for a minute. "You're trying to help me, aren't you? Do you want me to follow you? How strange…"

He ran forward once more and then stared back at her, cocking his head to one side. He felt Pippin motioning to her as well. As she was contemplating, Wilbur noticed a strange wispy figure looming above her. It was whispering, but shrieking at the same time.

"Come Wilbur, I know where Ernest is. Come with me. Bring the woman. The Will O The Wisp knows."

Wilbur's hairs stood on end, and every part of his body told him not to trust whatever it was. His hackles raised. The woman started to look frightened and started to turn towards where his gaze had gone. Wilbur thought quickly, and barked a few times more as friendly as he could manage. He spun in a little circle, keeping the wisp in his sights. The woman seemed to relax again.

"Okay, well I suppose there's no harm in trying…" The woman smiled, dusted off her hat, and hesitantly followed behind Wilbur and Pippin. As she followed, Wilbur looked back and noticed the wisp had gone.

As the giant willow tree finally came into view, Wilbur's heart raced. His tail bagan to wag. Pippin clung tightly. They all kept their eyes forward as they pushed through the haze and weeds. Silhouettes of people began to appear through the fog. They were talking amongst themselves and slowly gathering around the tree. There were more people than Wilbur could count. His nose was on the ground instantly. He knew Ernest's smell better than anybody. If he was here, he would find him. The woman though very taken aback, seemed to understand why they'd brought her. She thanked them profusely before she split off into the crowd in search of her son. Wilbur's senses were overloaded. The smells were intense and everywhere all at once. The willow tree itself smelled like wood aged over thousands of years, and the flowers that grew around it were as sweet as a warm summer day. Pippin played look-out at the highest point of Wilbur's back. They could still hear the woman faintly calling for Peter, and they kept an eye out for him as well. Every once in a while, Wilbur saw the wisp. It was hovering, as if it were waiting for someone. It made him uneasy.

The voices of the crowd became louder and louder. Names were being shouted from every direction. People of every size and shape were running this way and that. It was all very strange, and Wilbur wondered how everybody had found their way here. As he approached the south-facing edge of the tree he saw a tall man in a flat cap... he did a double take and his heart skipped a beat. Intently, he picked up the pace. This had to be Ernest... it had to be. His best friend in the entire world was there in front of him once again. He could already feel the warm embrace. He felt Pippin shiver with excitement, and he knew he'd seen him too. As he got within greeting distance, a little boy raced over, cutting off his path. His arms outstretched. Before Wilbur could think the little boy was already upon him, hanging around his neck and rubbing him on the nose.

Wilbur tried to look around the boy to keep Ernest in his sight. He noticed the wisp, it hung above Ernest's head like a ghost. Wilbur tried to break free, but the little boy clung on tightly. Briefly, he looked down at the boy. He couldn't have been more than four years old, and he was terrified. Wilbur's heart sank for him. He gave him a small lick and let his gaze peel fully away from Ernest and the wisp. As the little thing crouched down to a sit, Wilbur noticed him adjust a small gold "P" pin on his coat pocket. Peter.... Wilbur knew immediately. He glanced back one more time at the man who could only be Ernest standing only a few feet away. He was now disappearing into the fog, the wisp was floating back and forth above his head. Wilbur glanced back to Peter, who was staring up at him with big round eyes.

In one earth shattering moment, Wilbur turned away from the man, and grabbed Peter gently by the edge of his coat, tugging him forward. Peter was giggling and stumbling along as Wilbur guided him through the masses of people. "Please wait for me Ernest, please." he said aloud. Which only came out as a small whimper. The toddling boy had happily grabbed hold of Pippin, who he was now carrying in one arm. Wilbur quickly tracked down the woman's scent, she was standing in a large circle of yellow flowers. He gave her a gentle shove with his snout and she spun around with a gasp of relief.

"Peter!!!" Bursting into tears she bent down to hug her son tightly, who squirmed with annoyance and affection all at once. Pippin squirmed too, and Wilbur realized his friend had been caught in the middle. He shook his head and sighed at the sight of his smooshed friend.

"Thank you ever so much!" The woman exclaimed, sweetly she reached for Pippin and replaced him on top of Wilbur's back. "Sorry about squishing you little thing." She patted Pippins tiny head. "I cannot thank you two enough... you're something special." Her smile would not cease, tears streaming down both cheeks. Wilbur sat and wagged his tail to say *you're welcome*. Peter broke from her grasp and rushed over to hug Wilbur one more time, burying his face into his fluffy chest. Wilbur gave him a small lick, and then nudged him back to his mother. It felt good to have helped someone, but it was time to help himself now.

"Best of luck to both of you, thank you again. I don't think I could ever repay you... I'll try and think of something, but we must be off now. I hope you find who you're looking for." She said tenderly, and gave a small wave. She grabbed Peter's hand, and they slowly disappeared into the fog. Wilbur watched them go and his heart ached. He missed Ernest more than ever. Once he knew they were safe, his nose was straight on the ground again. He sniffed every shoe, and eyed every flat cap. He quickly made his way back to where he saw the man. Half closing his eyes, he peered around the tree.

The man was long gone, and so was the wisp. His heart sank to the bottom of his chest. The sun cast a gloomy purple and red glow as it started to set. He began to see the same faces over and over... but none of them were Ernest. He couldn't will his body to move. All he could bring himself to do was stand there and watch. He watched as the crowd started to find each other, recognizing loved ones, hugging, kissing, and then they started to dissipate. Pippin was still very quiet as Wilbur sat down in the middle of the clearing, defeated. The fog came in thick again, surrounding everything in sight. Wilbur slowly stood and walked back toward the ancient willow with his tail between his legs. He fell onto the ground with a heartbreaking thud. He was at a loss. Pippin slid down and put his tiny paw over Wilbur's, his captain's hat crumpled at his side.

"I really thought he was going to be here Pippin... I don't know what to do. I trusted Rell... And did you see that wispy creature? What if it got Ernest?" Pippin didn't respond, he just sat and rubbed Wilbur's paw trying to comfort him. "We need to get out of this forest. Nothing makes sense here. There's a good chance Ernest went to a village nearby, and hopefully he stayed there, but we have to get out of here Pippin. This place is impossible. I'm starting to wonder if anybody here truly knows how to help. My heart can't take it." He sighed and laid his large head next to his tiny friend.

"I am sorry Wilbur really... this is all my fault." Pippin said sadly, playing with his long ears.

"It isn't your fault Pip... but why wouldn't he wait for me? Do you think he gave up on me? Why did Rell tell me to help when I can? I did... and what did that get me?" Wilbur's eyes welled up.

"He most certainly did not give up on you Wilbur." The little rabbit sounded very indignant as he inched closer. He hugged Wilbur with all of his tiny might, a few tears trickled down his little pink nose.

"How are you so certain?" Wilbur said with another saddened sigh, his ears fell flat against his head.

"There's something I should tell you." Pippin whispered, barely loud enough for Wilbur to hear.

"Can I be of any service?" A strange voice interrupted.

Wilbur and Pippin simultaneously turned their heads toward the sound. A fox had slipped silently through the mist. He was the deepest shade of red, almost crimson rather than orange with eyes of fire to match. He stood there and magnificently blended into the setting sun. "I apologize for the intrusion, but I overheard your despair. It is as heavy as the fog around us. What is it that you seek Wilbur? I am here to guide those who find the willow, and I can try my best if you'll allow it. The name is Leer." His voice fell like deep satin across the dirt and leaves. The branches of the willow swayed and framed him like a painting.

Pippin curled up silently behind Wilbur's haunch, jittering with nerves. Wilbur inched backwards. He stared in reverence as a warm glow surrounded the being and his blood-red fur. Wilbur was still unsure, but this, this had to be a god. He breathed deeply and quietly as if trying not to offend the creature. He gathered his story once again. As he began to explain, his vision drifted, and he thought he saw a small black tail waving in the distance.

Chapter

Eleven

Ernest approached the door of Maeve's cozy little cottage. As he gently pushed open the sage green door, the smell of fresh bread greeted him in a warm embrace. The lovely cottage was nearly two hundred years old, and Ernest couldn't help but admire it every time he stepped inside. There was a hearth to the far end of the sitting room, its mantlepiece adorned with a variety of hanging herbs. Directly left of the sitting room was a dark wooden staircase that lead up to two small bedrooms and a quaint bathroom. To the right was the kitchen, full of natural light, and more often than not, enchanting smells. The whole place was adorned with mystical little trinkets and tokens from a lifetime of adventures It was a place that a faerie could call home.

"Well it's quite cozy in here today isn't it?" Ernest smiled as he approached Maeve and gave her a comforting hug from behind.

"I'd have to agree with you on that one." She paused to face him and return his smile. "I've made lots of progress!" She said, spreading her hands wide to display the array of treats and food that lined her counters. Ernest let her go and she spun around like an excited child in a sweet shop. He inspected her hard work.

"Rather impressive, are these really homemade dog treats?" Ernest picked up a small biscuit in the shape of a paw print. He peered at it hard and feigned disbelief.

"Of course they are!" She gave him a flustered look and grabbed the biscuit from his hands, holding it proudly up to the sunlight. "It really isn't that hard, I just omitted some things from your traditional shortbread recipe, and then added a few magic ingredients..." Maeve smiled as she gestured to the giant jar of peanut butter sitting near the stove. She tossed the small biscuit back onto its pile.

"Oh sweet Maeve...How long have you been awake?" Ernest asked with a playfully raised eyebrow.

"Uhhh... since about five o'clock this morning." She looked around admiring her valiant effort once more. She turned to the counter and began to roll out even more dough, when suddenly smoke started to billow from the oven. "Shoot! The bacon rolls!" Maeve dusted her hands off on her dark green pinny and ran to the oven in a graceful huff. Ernest just shook his head sweetly. He grabbed the rolling pin and picked up where she had left off with the dough.

"Just in time! Only a tad bit on the crispy side." She exclaimed, blowing a fallen curl away her brow.

"This is wonderful, but have you overdone it a bit do you think? He's not an elephant." Ernest teased.

Maeve playfully rolled her eyes. "Nonsense, more food means more smells. More smells means we will be easier for Wilbur to find." She said pridefully. "Now where is that list of his favorite treats, do you still have it with you?"

"Maeve... do you really think this will work?" He paused his rolling and turned to her. Maeve just looked at him confidently and shushed him. Ernest smiled and reached into his pocket. He handed her a small crumpled piece of paper. She read it off quietly.

"Peanut butter biscuits, bacon, cheese, and strawberry scones." Maeve smiled tenderly, taking pleasure in the fact that Ernest felt a bit embarrassed. "Well, the good news is, I have everything done besides the scones! We will have to run into town and see if there are any strawberries, but first tea."

"Tea is always first!" Ernest agreed.

Maeve turned to put the kettle on while Ernest finished rolling out the last of the dough. He pinched a small bit off the end and shyly tasted it. He was surprised by how pleasant it was. "You know, you'd make a good bit of money if you sold these treats at the inn!"

"That's not a bad thought... If I can find the time. You'll have to help me write down all the recipes later." The cupboards rattled as she searched for her tea set.

"Hey... I'm capable of good ideas too." He said giving her a look over his shoulder. They both laughed and Maeve turned to give him a teasing pat on the back. She gathered the tea tray together and took it to the table in the front garden. Ernest wiped his hands and followed.

They sat together with their tea taking in the views of the immaculate garden. The permeating Spring air had woken up the snowdrops and the bluebells, and they bashfully began to poke their heads out of the surrounding soil. The air was sweet and inviting. As Ernest turned his gaze back to Maeve he noticed that she had a very serious face on.

"What are you thinking about?" He asked.

"Well... I don't know it seems silly." She stared down at the table.

"What do you mean? I don't think anything can surprise me now."

"Well... I mean once we find Wilbur because I know we will. When do you plan on going home...As in leaving?" Maeve looked down into her tea and swirled it.

"Actually... I was going to talk to you about that. I was wondering if you'd like the idea of me... well us... Wilbur and I, sticking around? We could use a change of scenery." He said trying to gauge if he was being too forward.

Maeve's face lit up and a huge smile played across her lips. She nervously played with her mustard yellow dress. "I would rather enjoy that I think…"

Ernest smiled and touched her hand. "I found a graveyard the day I got lost in the forest, it seems like it would be a good option for me if I stayed. I could transfer or just change jobs entirely, and of course, help you with the inn if you needed it. I've seen lots of homes available to buy as well, and I know Wilbur will love it here as much as I do. I really do think change could do some good, especially after everything that has happened." He looked at her with eyes that precariously balanced love and terror.

Maeve squeezed his hand with a reassuring grasp. She looked happy, but he knew she could feel his fear. Her warm brown eyes hinted at a tear, but she smiled. "I couldn't agree more. I was trying to be strong, but I didn't want to have to say goodbye… and I can help however you need. I know it'll be a big shift for you, but the man who owns the graveyard is so kind. I could introduce you, and I'm sure he could use the help." They sat hand in hand for a while. "I just sort of want to see where this goes… You, Wilbur, and I." She said through a shy smile.

Ernest gave her a tender nod of agreement. Maeve slowly got up and gave Ernest a shy kiss on the forehead, and looked as if she thought she'd crossed a line. Her face became red, and Ernest beamed. She bit her lip and looked away from him. "We've got work to do." Her movements were flustered as she gathered the dishes and slowly made her way to the cottage.

Ernest trailed behind and gathered a few flowers. When he entered the kitchen he grabbed an empty teapot and filled it with water. He placed the bundle of flowers in it delicately. He could see Maeve's faint smile behind her broom handle as she swept up.

"You know... I have two bedrooms here. Plenty of space... I wouldn't mind if you and Wilbur wanted to stay here while you got your feet on the ground. As long as you pick flowers for me every day." She flashed him a sheepish smile. Ernest leaned against the counter and pretended to ponder the offer.

"You really don't have to do that... but I'd be happy accept those conditions. As long as Wilbur fancies you... You can be a bit of a troublemaker sometimes." He gave her a mischievous grin.

Maeve smiled and rolled her eyes as she continued sweeping. He went over and put the last bit of biscuit dough into the fridge to chill. "I'll phone James tomorrow and see what I can sort out. After we find Wilbur... if we find Wilbur."

"We will Ernest." She floated over and handed him his jacket. "Now let's see about some strawberries, shall we? We have lots to get done before tomorrow, and I cannot wait to meet Wilbur." She beamed and leaned her broom against the kitchen's pebbly wall, she approached Ernest and hooked his arm in hers. Playfully, they walked out the door and headed to town. As they walked down the winding streets Ernest noticed that some of his posters were missing. He swiftly unlinked Maeve's arm and veered over to the florist's shop.

"What is it Ernest?" Maeve asked, following closely behind.

"I swear I hung a poster here…" Ernest studied the old brick wall, his brow wrinkled in confusion.

Maeve came closer and inspected the wall as well. Ernest placed a hand where the nail had been. He spotted the florist woman inside.

"Excuse me miss, sorry but did you remove my dog poster?" He gently called through the doorway.

The woman dawned a fancy white hat. She was heavy set and her cheeks were blushed from bustling about. She wiped her hands on her blue and white dress and approached the storefront.

"Oh dear, no I didn't! I didn't even notice it was gone when I opened up the shop this morning. Don't think it would've been the street cleaners…" She looked flustered as she thought about it.

"How odd, right thank you miss, sorry to bother. Maybe it was the wind." He tried to sound convinced.

"No problem dearie, you have a nice day. I'll keep a lookout." She waved them off politely, and quickly got back to arranging her chrysanthemums.

Ernest scratched his chin as they walked. As they rounded the street corner, Ernest saw that the poster he'd placed on the bus stop had vanished as well. He and Maeve paused. They exchanged a worried glance, before hesitantly walking on.

CHAPTER TWELVE

Wilbur finished telling his tale and Leer leaned in closer. He studied Wilbur closely and then Pippin who still shook nervously against Wilbur's haunch. The primordial fox closed his eyes and sat in silence for a while. Wilbur looked around worriedly. Pippin peered up at him, still barely daring to move.

Finally Leer spoke, his liquid voice broke through the clouds of fog and seemed to come down like rain around them. "I want you to leave this forest tomorrow."

Wilbur was shocked, his head turned involuntarily to the side. He remained silent and hoped Leer would explain.

"Tomorrow is the equinox of Spring. The fog will lift, and you will be able to make your exit. Go East. You will find a village. Your Ernest is there. I have seen it." His voice rolled across the tall grass and the soft green blades bent forward, as if bowing to this god-like creature. Wilbur felt tears burning in the corners of his eyes. He still could not speak. He felt Pippin nudge him in excitement. "Please be careful, everything is not always as it seems outside these forest walls." The fox's gaze seemed to snap back to the present moment, and he looked tenderly at Wilbur. "Until tomorrow, I have a den near here that is empty. You and your small friend can stay there. You'll be safe and dry." Leer stretched out a paw and pointed toward the den. He said nothing more. He only closed his eyes wearily as if all of his energy had just been expelled.

"Thank you... thank you so much. I will repay you however I can." Wilbur waited for a response but it did not come. He started to walk away in the direction the fox had pointed, but couldn't help stealing one last look at the blood-red fox sitting as a statue descended from some other world. Pippin's little feet pattered behind and he quickly climbed back up onto Wilbur's back. They headed towards the small den.

"Do you think this is it Pippin? Leer said he saw Ernest, but how? Can I really leave this place so easily? It all seems so impossible, but I also didn't think I could talk until now, so maybe anything is possible? What about you? Can I still come visit you?" Wilbur couldn't stop his questions, and he was trying his hardest not to let his excitement overtake him. It all felt so real, but so dream-like at the same time. Could he really trust Leer? He felt Pippin sag deeper into a sit.

His little voice came quiet, and with what Wilbur detected as a tinge of melancholy. "I think that whatever that fox says… is probably true. I've never seen anything like him…But are you sure you want to leave? Maybe we should wait a few days?"

"I can't wait anymore Pip… plus I don't think I'll ever find my way out if I don't try tomorrow. This fog is relentless, and if it really does lift I need to take my chance." The wagging of his tail began to slow as his worries grew.

"Okay I understand. If it's okay I think maybe I'll stay here tomorrow. I can always wait for you to come back… I should probably get back to Violet anyways." Pippin said, the sadness in his voice wasn't easily hidden this time.

"I'm sorry Pip. I know this means I have to leave, but I promise I'll come back to visit. I'll always come visit, you're my friend, and I'd really like you to meet Ernest. I think you'd really get on well." Wilbur let a small smile sneak out. "Hey, maybe I could convince him to let you and Violet live with us, wouldn't that be great? We have plenty of room, and you'd be safe and warm." His tail wagged fast now and his ears perked up for the first time in a long time. His eagerness began to spread through him like a wildfire, but Pippin stayed quiet and only squeezed Wilbur tightly.

They eventually came to a tree with a large hollow at the bottom. "This must be it." Wilbur said, half to himself. It was the perfect size for a good cozy sleep. Pippin climbed in first and arranged some moss at the back edge, his ears were low and his face downtrodden. Wilbur shimmied in after and circled until he felt fit. He hunkered down with his head near the edge of the hollow. He scooted back closer to Pippin in order to keep him warm, and stretched out a back paw to rest against the little rabbit. He only wanted to comfort him. Wilbur began to doze and then perked up once more.

"Pippin? Are you awake?" He asked softly.

"Yeah I'm awake." Pippin replied softly.

"I just remembered, what did you want to tell me before? At the willow tree? You were interrupted." He asked closing his eyes again.

"It's nothing, we need to sleep. It's a big day tomorrow." His voice came out weak and squeakier than usual.

"Are you alright? You seem really down lately. Is it because I have to leave? Or is there something else?" Wilbur asked sleepily.

"I'm alright Wilbs, we can talk more tomorrow...Oh and... I love you Wilbur."

Wilbur smiled through tired eyes. "I love you too Pip, you're a great friend." Wilbur yawned and left it at that. His breathing fell into the rhythmic moss-covered silence that surrounded them. He let himself give into his imagination. He pictured tomorrow, running into Ernest's warm embrace once again. The roast dinners, the long drives, the warm hearth after a hard day's work. There was still enough Spring left for them to count the lambs as well. He couldn't wait. The sweet memories crowded in and guided him down a peaceful path to sleep.

IN THE DEAD OF THE NIGHT, WILBUR STARTED TO stir. His nose wouldn't stop twitching. He reluctantly opened one sleepy eye. Something smelled strangely familiar. He slowly opened both eyes and looked around trying to locate the source of the scent. In the pitch black it was hard to distinguish anything at all. Quietly, as to not wake Pippin who was finally asleep, Wilbur stood up and walked out of the hollow. He cautiously sniffed around the edge of the tree. Where was it coming from? His nose lead him to a bed of dandelions, the strange scent was now mixing with the florals and the rain-soaked ground. The mud was cold and uninviting on his tired paws.

The old tree creaked in the wind. Wilbur's ears swiveled this way and that. The scent was so strong, yet so muddled. After sniffing around for a long while he found nothing but cold night air. He decided to head back towards the tree. The scent still lingered heavily in his nose. As he reached the trail leading up to the hollow, the source presented itself. A black cat, sitting in the middle of the path. Before he could react, the cat spoke.

"Wilbur I'm assuming? You need to come with me. Please don't be a dumb and ask questions. You dogs tend to do that, and we really don't have the time. My name is Pendle... and you have been utterly lied to." He spoke very confidently. In an accent Wilbur couldn't place, but pleasantly sharp.

Wilbur watched as Pendle walked briskly past him. Tail held in a question mark. The strange cat didn't even look back to see if Wilbur was following. Wilbur had a quick peek into the hollow, Pippin was still sound asleep. He swiftly turned around and followed the cat. As they walked on into the cool night air, Wilbur tried hard to keep his questions to himself. Who had lied to him? How did he know this cat was the one telling the truth? It was all very worrying. There was a chill in the air that whispered in his ears and crept down his spine. It made him shiver. Part of him wanted to turn around and go back to sleep. He just wanted to see Ernest in what was probably only a few hours from now. Despite his reservations, he continued on in fraught silence keeping that punctual tail in his sights.

They soon passed the giant willow, and after a while Wilbur noticed that they were walking alongside a familiar river. It shun like a dream in the moonlight. He began to recognize many of the surroundings. He had been through all of these places before. Where on Earth was this cat taking him? Nose to the ground, Wilbur was intent on getting to the bottom of this peculiar turn of events. Every once in a while, the faint scent of a rabbit tickled Wilbur's nose. He turned around each time almost hoping to see Pippin shyly following, but there was only darkness.

Chapter Thirteen

Pippin awoke with a start. He hopped up and spun around, frantically searching the dark hollow for Wilbur. He was alone and it was very cold. He carefully stepped out of the big tree and scanned the dark surroundings. Wilbur had never left him like this... something was very wrong. As he peered along the path, he could just make out some faint tracks in the dirt. They were Wilbur's, but there was another set as well. He must have been following someone. Pippin pressed his small pink nose to the ground. An eerily familiar smell accosted his nose.

"Pendle!" He gasped to himself. He needed to find them and fast. As he swiftly turned to go back for his rucksack he collided with a large creature. Falling onto his little cotton tail, Pippin hesitantly looked up. He met the piercing ember gaze of Leer.

His low voice tore through the eerie silence. "We need to follow Wilbur. Something is wrong, and I do believe there are things you have yet to tell me small one. I would suggest you do that now."

Pippin tremored from both the cold and his fear. He looked shamefully down at the dirt and tugged at his long ears. He slowly got up and retrieved his rucksack without uttering a single sound. When he returned, he found Leer in a dignified bow, nose touching the Earth in perfect posture. He made his way over to the fox and awkwardly climbed onto his back. For a while, there was only the hush of the midnight forest. Pippin's small voice eventually peeked through the silence. He had decided to come clean. Leer turned back his ears and listened intently as they walked on into the night.

CHAPTER
Fourteen

Wilbur's nose was engulfed in familiar smells. So much so that he started to become uneasy. He couldn't quite place where they had come to, but he knew it was important. He swore that he could smell Ernest and weirdly himself as well... there was a lingering scent of iron intermingling with dirt. As he wildly sniffed around, Pendle sat off to the side and watched. It was as if he was waiting for Wilbur to discover something.

His nose took him to the edge of the forest. It all started to come back to him, as he looked up through the moonlit fog a large yew tree emerged. It was illuminated by the eerie yellow moonlight, whic revealed a large crack in the front of its trunk. Wilbur was overcome with emotion as he thought of that fateful day, of Ernest. He ran full tilt toward the tree. As he reached the forest's edge, a powerful force of wind sent him sprawling back. He tried again and again, but every time he was flung backward, as if there were a giant invisible wall. Wilbur whined in despair and turned quickly to face Pendle with a frenzied look in his eyes.

"Please help me... I don't understand! What is going on? Why did you bring me here?"

With a tilt of his small black head, Pendle motioned Wilbur to follow once again. He walked further on into the wood. Wilbur trailed behind anxiously. They came to a grove of low-hanging trees, and Pendle positioned himself purposely underneath the friendliest looking one. Wilbur finally caught up and saw that there was something large lying at the cat's feet. A foul smell attacked his nose, something old, something earthy. Wilbur carefully got closer, and then he froze. Pendle's face gave way to a somber expression. His pointed ears flattened against his head, and he stepped to the side as if to give Wilbur a moment. Wilbur couldn't move, he couldn't cry, he couldn't even make a noise. Lying under that friendly tree, was Wilbur himself. Cold, wet, and most definitely lifeless. He didn't fall asleep that day he ran from the car... he died.

"No... no no this can't be. This can't be! This can't be real... I'm here... I'm right here. No... Pendle... no.."
Wilbur's eyes burned with tears, as he stared at himself

motionless in the soft grass. He grasped at his surroundings for answers, spinning toward Pendle who only looked away in anguish. Wilbur felt the sensation rising in him once again, he had to run and he did, he ran faster than he ever had... away from Pendle and into the suffocating mist. "No... no... no" He repeated the only words he could seem to force out. He couldn't trust anyone anymore, not even Pippin. Another wave of panic set in as he wondered how he was going to get out of the forest. He was panting hard and the ground thudded under his ghostly paws. Anger and sadness rushed through him like a torrential flood. He felt betrayed and alone.

There had to be some way to reverse this... some way for him to be back with Ernest once again. Ernest... he still had to find Ernest no matter what, but the thought of him finding out that Wilbur was...well...gone was too much for him to bear. "Ernest! Ernest!" He called over and over as shrill whimpers and cries rang out through desolate forest. The tears splashed back against his face in the wind. He ran until he reached the eastern edge of the forest as Leer had suggested. The fog was still thicker than ever. He knew he was too early, but he decided he would try his luck anyways. If he could get out, would he be alive again? Was it that simple?

He closed his eyes and sprinted toward the treeline... a street and a graveyard peered over a hill in the distance. As he reached the edge, he was slammed backwards with an unrelenting force just like before. Wilbur tried over and over, skidding back against the dirt try after try. He was exhausted, his chest heaved and the tears stained his white speckled muzzle. With one more deep breath, he mustered up a final attempt... he burst forward with all of his might. He was met with a huge crash and a flash of light as he flew through the air straight back into the damp dark forest. He sailed through the mist and pummeled into the hard ground below with a sharp whimper. His nose filled with dirt as his face slid across the harsh ground. His vision faded into darkness.

Wilbur awoke... he was on the other side of the treeline now. He had made it through the barrier after all. He felt alive! He ran with his nose to the ground and sped along stony cobbled streets. The wonderful smells of civilization littered the air. Best of all, he could smell Ernest and he was close. He came to a small inn and without thinking he burst through the doors. His fluffy black and white tail wagged more than ever as he ran down the hall. Finally, he came to a door and found Ernest sitting on a rickety old bed. Ernest turned to face him. His face immediately lit up... like an angel descended from the heavens. Wilbur bounded over to him and jumped onto the bed. He licked Ernest from head to shoulders. Ernest embraced him warmly and fully the same way he had when they first met, Wilbur a small bumbly puppy. This time Ernest wouldn't ever let go. He was home, he was safe, he was alive. They would never let go.

THE UNDERTAKER AND HIS DOG

"Heeeeee... heeeee... shooo" A faded voice squeaked in the distance.

Wilbur's eyes creaked open, a sleepy haze clouded his vision and Ernest floated away like dust in the breeze. The forest around him came in and out the blackness as he struggled to stay awake. He felt himself move an inch or so across the ground... He craned his neck to look behind him.

"Shoo... man... okay come on Pip... You can do this."

He felt himself move another inch. As his vision started to clear, he saw a small rabbit running back and forth from his rear paws to the scruff of his neck. Back and forth, back and forth. With every effort he was pulling and moving Wilbur a speck at a time. Until finally the little thing collapsed and wiped his paw along his forehead.

"Wilbur?... are you still in there?"

The words sounded far away to Wilbur's ears. He was so dizzy, it felt as if he were swimming. "...Pippin?" He tried to squeeze out a sound. He saw a faint smile cross Pippin's round cheeks.

"It's me, Wilbur... I'm here for you. I know you might be mad... but."

In a split second Wilbur shot up on his feet. He was burning with anger. He bared his teeth as he swiftly went down toward Pippin with a snarl. The helpless rabbit let out a shriek. He covered his eyes with his ears and cowered into the rock behind him. As he looked out from behind his ears, his big round eyes were full of genuine terror. He was shaking horribly. Wilbur immediately felt ashamed. He was angry but this wasn't him. He backed off quickly and turned his back to Pippin.

"Wilbur... I... I am so sorry. I have no excuse. I just wanted a friend."

"Pippin... you wasted my time. You wanted a friend and you cost me my only one! You knew I would never find Ernest. You knew!" He felt the sting of his words as they escaped.

Pippin tried to respond, his voice trembling with tears. "I know... but there's a chance you could still find him... if we just listen to Leer."

"Listen to Leer?! He's probably a complete loon, like the rest of you in this god forsaken forest. Ernest and I are separated forever, Pippin... Why did I have to run off and die? Why did I abandon him? I have been dead for days now Pippin... I am lying under a tree dead!" Wilbur slumped to the ground still turned away from his friend. As he looked around, the forest began to feel like a hellscape. The gnarled grey branches reached towards him, as if they wanted to trap him forever. Everything was covered in dark grey fog. Wilbur's heart felt like it had broken into a million pieces. Nothing would ever be the same. He sank down lower and sobbed.

"We can still find him, Wilbur... I know it sounds impossible, but I know there has to be a way." Pippin's voice was faint. Wilbur knew he felt bad.

"Even if this equinox plan works, I'm still dead. It won't ever be the same." His voice melted into a numbness. Pippin could only be silent. He cautiously approached Wilbur, and sat near enough to brush his fur with his own. "How did you and Violet get your scars?" Wilbur asked suddenly.

"Pardon?"

"How did you and your sister get your scars? You're dead... I'm assuming that everyone here is. How did you die?" He asked once more, a touch of softness returning to his voice.

Pippin's words fell out nervously. "Oh... right. Well... um... it was a long time ago now. I remember it being a beautiful sunny day. There was a warm breeze and the birds sounded so happy in the trees. I could feel an adventure rounding the bend, and I knew Violet felt it too. She begged me to take her down to the river so we could play, and of course I obliged. As we walked I became aware that we had strayed quite far from our hutch. A feeling of worry washed over me, but I didn't want ruin our day. She looked so peaceful and happy, chasing the butterflies down the stream." Pippin bit his lip and looked down into the dirt, a few beats of silence passed. "I always did my best to keep her safe. Truly I did, but that day it wasn't enough." Wilbur stayed silent, he finally looked back at Pippin. He shimmied back, and placed a paw gently on Pippins little foot.

"We built a little mushroom fort, and we played kings and queens, but we both started to get hungry. I told Violet to wait further up the bank away from the water while I went further down river to forage some snacks. I began to rummage through the hedges for berries, and the next thing I knew... there was this blood-curdling scream. As I turned around I saw Violet being shaken around in the jaws of a massive badger. His teeth were huge and stained with yellow. I dropped everything and ran to her. I threw rocks, sticks, and anything I could to get him to let go. He did let go, but it was too late and then he came for me." Tears trickled down Pippin's tiny nose.

"We woke up in this forest, and we've been here ever since. We see souls come through day in and day out, looking for some sort of contented end to it all. If they achieve it, they seem to disappear. I can only hope there is some sort of wonderful afterlife, after this. If they don't find what they're looking for... they stay here. Ever since the badger... I have kept a promise to make sure Violet is safe no matter what. I think she hates me for it sometimes, and maybe there's no point since we are already dead, but I don't think I'll ever forgive myself. Everything I said to you when we met wasn't a lie... not the badger part at least." The little rabbit sighed heavily and rested himself against Wilbur's flank.

Wilbur looked at his friend, he could feel the heartbreak and regret like a thick balmy dew. Wilbur was quiet for a while. He wondered if he found Ernest, would he be fulfilled? Would he disappear? He felt Pippin lean in closer and try to get cozy, he knew his friend just wanted comfort.

"Did you have a human too?" Wilbur asked more tenderly.

"Mhmm... I only remember that she was lovely and tall. She was so kind to us. I don't like to think about it much... How sad we must've made her." He tugged his long velvety ears.

Wilbur sighed and gave Pippin a friendly nudge. "Did you drag me all the way over here by yourself?" He asked changing the subject.

"Yeah...it took quite a long time." Pippin tried to look exacerbated and giggled to himself. Wilbur couldn't help but snicker along. What a ridiculous creature this tiny rabbit was.

"Do you really think there's still hope Pip? Ernest... he's the only thing in this world that I want. Even if it's only for a fleeting moment... and if I truly can't be with him again... then at least I'd like to end his heartache if only to bring about another one." He felt the tears coming through again. His heart fell deeper into his chest with every word. He was going to break his best friend.

"Well... I think come evening on the Spring equinox, we listen to Leer. See if you can get out of here and go from there. I would still like to go home to Violet, if that's alright. I'm worried about her." He looked down again, and Wilbur gave him a reassuring nod. "It seems like you know where you're going by now. There's no need for your captain anymore, and I think it's your only option Wilbs. Violet and I will always keep a lookout for you."

"Okay..." He replied lying his head down in a heaving sigh. He felt Pippin snuggle in again.

A soft whisper escaped. "I am so sorry Wilbur... you are my greatest friend. I just didn't want you to disappear."

"I won't disappear Pip... and I am sorry too about before, and about you and Violet."

They both closed their eyes. Trying to get some semblance of rest while they could. Wilbur clenched his jaw as the golden light of dawn began to dance through the trees.

He smiled and whispered "By the way, I'll always need my captain."

Chapter Fifteen

Ernest shuffled into the cottage and laid down the burlap sacks of groceries with a huff. Maeve followed closely behind and began unpacking the lot. There was an uncomfortable silence. Ernest could feel that he was trying to force himself to speak. Nothing came out. He stared blankly at the produce that fell out of the sacks. It tumbled clumsily across the chestnut table.

"Hey, Ern… Are you alright? You've been awfully quiet since we left the market." Maeve spoke in a soft tone as she nervously washed some apples at the sink.

"I just… my whole life has changed in the blink of an eye Maeve. I lost my best friend, I haven't been at work, and I barely remember what my own home looks like anymore. Most of all I am so scared that this picnic idea isn't going to work. I just want Wilbur." He knew he was avoiding eye contact, but everything felt impossible. "Plus the fact that our posters seem to be vanishing into thin air."

"I understand, and I know this is a lot for you. I'm sure the posters are due to the rough weather. It happens all the time, but we can definitely look into it." She paused at the sink and stared distractedly at one of the shining red apples. She continued with a tone that sounded almost hurt. "And you don't have to move here... if you'd rather go back home I would support you. I could always visit... I didn't mean to change the whole course of your life."

Ernest could tell she was sad and only wanted to be supportive. He stood silently for a while longer and then slowly gazed over at Maeve standing in her yellow dress. Her soft brown eyes were illuminated by the sun coming through the kitchen window. She was bathed in gold. Her curls falling out across her face. There was a sad but strong expression as she polished the apples with gentle hands. Again he had the vision of her, a sweet and graceful deer standing in the forest. Standing so still as if not wanting to upset the nature around her. A smile started to split his mouth against his will.

"Maeve... I think that's exactly what was supposed to happen." He beamed at her as he walked over to help her wash the produce. She smiled, relieved, and blushed heavily.

"I know that this might not work Ernest, but what have we got to lose? It's something, isn't it? At least we can say we've tried everything."

Ernest grabbed an apple from her and began putting it into the bowl with the rest of the fruit. He stared at it and contemplated. "Yeah, you're right. I'd do anything and everything for him. I just hope he knows that."

"He does Ernest." Maeve said sweetly. She began putting ingredients together for the strawberry scones.

"I just don't know why he hasn't come into the village. He is so smart Maeve. Surely he would know to come toward people." Ernest's face melted into a worried frown.

"Ernest, you know that forest. You know firsthand how impenetrable it can be. There's a good chance he's tried, and hopefully he'll try again tomorrow." She dusted off her flour-covered hands and lightly clasped them around Ernest's face. "We are going to find him... No matter what it takes or how long. He's around somewhere I can feel it in my bones." She smiled confidently. It seemed to rub off on Ernest.

"Okay." He smiled and grabbed her hands in his.

"How did you ever become so stubborn?" Ernest teased.

"Correction... determined." She gave him a teasing look back. "What can I say. I had a hard life... but I never gave up on anything I believed in. My father left when I was very young, he sends me money sometimes to help with the inn, but rarely. He sort of just said goodbye and the inn landed in my lap. I of course love it to death, but it takes a damn determined soul. And as far as my mother, she passed away a few months after I was born. I have one photo to serve as a memory of her, one. Ernest, I have been alone in this world since I can remember." She paused and softly touched the silver locket around her neck. "In all honesty my only friend until you showed up has been Uncle Ben, but despite everything, I have never lost my heart. I also have never been one to let a lost soul struggle. This brings us here… You are a lost soul Ernest and I will not let you give up until your soul breaks through and shines brightly once again."

A focused grin flashed across her soft face. Her eyes becoming glassy, stared deep into his. "You have a lot of light left in there, and to tell you the truth my soul is a lot less lost now too…" She smiled with a certain conviction. A small tear graced the corner of her eye. She quickly wiped it away and turned back to the scones.

Ernest mustered up the courage, and embraced her in a tight hug from behind. He held her for a long time. He knew in some strange way, they needed each other, and he didn't know how to say that he was proud of her. He felt it wasn't his place. "I'm going to head over to the phone box to see about selling my house. I know a few people who may be interested. Don't burn this one down while I'm gone. We might need it." He smiled as he heard a small giggle.

"Get your stuff from the inn while you're out. I can't have you taking up a room over there anymore. I suppose you can set up here from now on... we can figure something out." She smiled coyly and Ernest returned it.

As he walked out the door he couldn't help but look for any sign of Wilbur. Still nothing. Walking down the lane, he noticed one of the remaining lost dog signs barely clinging to a stone wall. It looked very weary and torn. The beautiful drawing was beginning to fade. Ernest grabbed it and unfurled the edges. As he stared at it, the tears started to burn and play within his eyes.

"Come on Wilbur. I need you. Please show up tomorrow...please." He stared out into the rolling hills, and crumpled the soggy drawing. He thought about throwing it in the bin. Instead, he shoved it into the breast pocket of his coat and gave it a small pat. Ernest arrived at the inn and made his way into the original phone box he had found days before. As he talked with a realtor, the pitter-patter of raindrops became louder and louder against the glass.

He would need to phone James as well, but he wanted to put it off as long as possible. He knew he would be sad to see him go. Ernest decided that he'd phone him as soon as he found Wilbur, to soften the blow with some good news. He walked slowly through the rain and climbed the old stone stairs into the inn. He made his way to his room and gathered all of his things into a rucksack. Before he left, he turned to the original drawing of Wilbur hanging in the dim light of that ancient room. Just above where he had slept. He went to rip it off but stopped.

"I'm going to leave you here my friend. Hopefully, somebody will come in here and know where you are. That's all I can do now... hope." He held his hand on the drawing and took a deep breath. Slowly, he gathered his rucksack and headed back to the cottage. As he walked down the stairs, a strange man hurried past him. He looked intense, and almost angry. Ernest looked at him and the man shot him a harsh glance. He shoved passed and threw the doors of the inn open. Ernest tried to shrug it off as he walked on. Tomorrow was a very important day.

CHAPTER SIXTEEN

"What the hell is the meaning of this?!" The man slammed a stack of torn posters onto the bar.

"Oh, Charles! You surprised me sir. I didn't know you were coming into town. Are you here to see Maeve?" Thomas asked as he finished wiping down the pint glasses.

"No I am not here to see Maeve, I leave this place to my only daughter and this is what we've become? Now I already asked you once... What is the meaning of these?!" He said again pointing an angry finger at the multitude of sketched border collie faces, they stared back with soft caramel eyes.

"Ah yes, Maeve drew that for a man in town. He was in a car accident nearby and lost his dog. They made these posters to spread the word. I do hope they find each other. It's an incredibly sad story really. The dog's name is Wilbur. Such a sweet face." Thomas smiled softly.

"I don't give a damn what the bloody dog's name is! These posters cannot be littering the street during my campaign." He walked over and threw them into the bin. He shot Thomas an impatient look.

"Campaign Sir?" Thomas' face became a scrunched look of concern.

"I'm running for mayor of Asphodel this autumn. Surprised you didn't hear. Now, leave please." Charles straightened his suit and slicked back his white hair. As he looked in the nearby mirror he seemed pleased with his stern expression.

Thomas worriedly put the pint glasses down. "Leave? We don't close for another hour."

"Leave... now. I have to start practicing my speech." He flashed Thomas a forced smile.

"Right sir, sorry, I'll be going then." Thomas slid the keys across the bar and quickly tidied up.

"Take the riff raff out with you as well please." Charles motioned to the three people that were enjoying their drinks.

"These riff raff are going to be your people... mayor." Thomas said sounding more than offended. Flustered, he brushed his bright red hair from his face. He gently gathered the people and politely asked them to leave. Charles rolled his eyes and waved them all away like flies crowding the air. As soon as everyone left he approached the mirror again.

"Ah yes my fellow Asphodelians, my name is Charles Reddington, I have held such a special place in my heart for you all for so long…" A rotten grin crept across his hardened face.

CHAPTER SEVENTEEN

As the sun started its long ascent into the blue Spring sky, Wilbur awoke. Today was the day. He would find Ernest and show him the truth. Wilbur's heart throbbed at the thought. He was about to replace his friend's despair with something far worse, but he knew that it was the only way. He took a deep breath and gently nudged Pippin who awoke with a squeak-like groan and rubbed his eyes.

"Is it time already?" Pippin asked, his sleepy voice getting lost in the warm breeze.

"I'm afraid so Pip." Wilbur stared into the ground.

"It's going to be okay Wilbur. You're doing the right thing." Pippin clambered up onto Wilbur's back and sat with a thump.

"I know, but sometimes I feel it would be easier if I didn't tell him. Then he could just forget about me." His heart fell in his chest like a lead balloon.

"The problem is that he wouldn't forget. Not ever. You know that Wilbs." His little friend's voice was soft and comforting. Wilbur felt Pippin's gentle strokes on his back. He knew that he was right, but the doubts in his head would not cease. He felt his little friend's head resting on the back of his own now. They were silent as Wilbur began their journey. The mist got thinner as every hour passed. The dirt felt cold and harsh under his paws. He noticed that the river's calming water now sounded shrill and loud in his ears. Even the rocks seemed to weep with a profound sadness. Drops of water rolled down their mossy faces. As they approached Pippin's home a raven landed in a tall cypress nearby. The branches moaned under its weight. It called out to them.

"The Yew tree! The Yew tree!" it croaked, in an unsettlingly human voice. Wilbur puzzled, cocked his head and opened his mouth to reply, but the large bird had already disappeared. His hairs bristled. He looked around the surrounding trees but the bird seemed to have vanished. He turned back to the tree house and slowly laid down near the the tiny familiar door. He didn't even notice Pippin climb down and go inside. He was in a daze as he mulled over the day ahead and the strange corvid. Startled out of his daydream, he focused in on Pippin and now Violet standing at the end of his nose. Violet immediately wrapped her arms around his snout entirely.

"Oh, Wilbur! I am so sorry. I thought you knew! I was so confused when I saw you last, I thought you knew why you were here, but then Pippin was giving me a look and then I wasn't sure what to tell you... and then... I can't believe Pippin lied to you! I can't imagine how you're feeling!" She shot a mean look at her brother followed by a light kick to his fluffy rump. Pippin gasped. Wilbur's mouth was still bound tightly, but the embrace was very much welcomed.

"Violet he can't talk, let go of him you ninny...and we already sorted things out." Pippin looked nervously at the dirt below, embarrassed.

"Oh right, I'm sorry...again." She quickly released Wilbur's muzzle and stepped back.

"That's quite alright, I think I was in need of the hug today." He replied kindly.

She nodded shyly and placed her paws behind her back. "Thank you for bringing my brother back safely... even if he is a pain." She said sweetly, giving Pippin another disapproving look. "Did you want us to come with you to find Ernest? We are at your service should you need us!" She stepped closer to Pippin who flinched as she gave a captain's salute.

"I appreciate the offer little one, but I need to do this alone." He gave them both a confident nod.

In an instant they were both upon him tightly hugging his big snout once more. Pippin's muffled voice came through.

"I am sorry Wilbur again for everything, but you are the bravest soul I know." He let go, as did Violet and they stared at him with big teary eyes.

"You are the bravest soul Pippin. Never forget that. In this life and in the last, and albeit a pain," He winked at Violet. "A wonderful friend as well." Their little rabbit sniffles began to surface as he nudged his nose into them gently. He had grown to love them genuinely, despite it all. He spoke with an almost false confidence. "I will see you both again soon. Be careful." They both backed away and nodded. Pippin wiped his little pink nose on the sleeve of his jacket. They each held a proud captain salute. As Wilbur slowly got up, he put a paw up to return their gesture. He turned his back to them and walked into the forest with uneasy steps. The trees seemed to grow closer and closer together as the fear closed in on him. A voice from somewhere unknown surprised him.

"It is almost time Wilbur."

He spun around. He recognized that voice.

"Over here dog."

Wilbur's eyes darted until he landed on the black cat sitting a few meters away. "Pendle?" The cat came forward slowly and sat next to him.

"Charmed... you're doing the right thing you know?" His bright green eyes gleamed in the light.

THE UNDERTAKER AND HIS DOG

Wilbur sat as well, and they stared down the path of endless trees. "So I am told... that doesn't make it any easier." He felt as if his stomach would burst at any second.

"I know." His tone was omnipotent.

"How can ripping my best friend's heart to pieces be the only way?" Wilbur's ears went flat against his head as the images of a broken Ernest raced through his mind.

"Because, by ripping it to pieces you are giving it the tools to repair itself." Returned Pendle.

Wilbur contemplated that for a moment. It felt as if Pendle could understand the entire world, as if it were as simple as a map laid in front of him. He turned to look at the strange cat sitting cool and collected, grooming his front paws. There were very faint bird calls in the distance, and Wilbur remembered the raven. "What is the importance of the Yew tree? Is there something I should know?"

"You've helped quite a few souls in this forest since you have arrived. You should understand that things like that don't go unnoticed here. The rest will come in time." His long black tail twitched side to side.

Wilbur felt lost. This place was a labyrinth with a riddle standing guard at every door. "Why is nothing ever straightforward here? I can't understand any of this." His voice was tired.

"It's the land of the dead. What exactly were you expecting?" Pendle raised a brow and turned a penetrating green eye toward Wilbur. Wilbur didn't know how to answer that. He just quietly stared back at the trees. "For now, you need to go. Ernest needs you, and that's all that matters. The equinox will reach its peak soon. Go toward the forest's edge nearest the village. I know you've been there once already."

Wilbur turned again toward the peculiar cat, but he had already walked away. He could just make out the question mark of his tail in the brush. Wilbur took a few minutes to gather himself. His breath felt like it was being cut short. He prayed to everything in the world that would listen. He needed courage. He needed strength. Finally, he stood up and started on his way again. As he walked along the forest floor, there was only himself, the neverending trees, and the maddening march of his ghostly heart.

To Wilbur's relief, the usual thick fog had indeed removed itself, and the view was clear as he finally approached the East edge of the forest. His mind flashed back to the day before. He trembled at the thought of being flung through the air again. His eyes stared nervously through the gaps in the trees. The familiar sight of tarmac gleamed at him in the sunlight just on the otherside. He took the deepest breath he could manage, closed his eyes, and put one paw in front of the other.

Immediately the ground changed underneath him. The warm pavement reached up to meet each paw pad. Something he had not felt in quite a while. Wilbur slowly opened his eyes. He made it. There was an eerie feeling, as if the forest behind him was reaching out in an attempt to pull him back in. He swore he heard the lilting voice of the Wisp, trying to lure him. He didn't look back. He felt alive. He made his way down cobbled streets as wonderfully familiar smells flooded his nose: bread, people, tea, other dogs, petrol, and finally Ernest. Wilbur slammed his nose to the ground and followed the trail intently. Out of the corners of his eyes, he saw children trying to greet him, he didn't have time today. He flashed quick looks with perked ears in their direction, but swiftly pressed on. The scent grew stronger every minute. His ears twitched as a stranger shouted "That's the dog on the sign!"

He didn't know what that meant, but he knew he was close to Ernest. That was all that mattered. His nose eventually bumped into a large stone step. Cautiously, he looked up. This was it. The inn from his hazy dream. He sprang up the steps and pummeled through the door, running head first into a large man. His paws skidded as he turned to get around him. He ran straight down the hall with the man yelling at his heels.

"What the?!!! Get the hell out of here!" The man desperately tried to grab him. Wilbur quickly ran into a bedroom...it was empty. This wasn't right, this isn't how it was supposed to be. Frantically, he searched every other room. Trunks of clothing fell among him in disarray, and his feet slid across the floors at every sharp turn. He ran back into what was supposed to be Ernest's room. Nothing. He was panting hard now. His eyes scanned every corner. How could this be? Ernest's smell was everywhere. The angry man flew into the room and Wilbur ran straight under his legs knocking a chair in front of him. The man fell hard on the floor swearing all the way down. The fiasco bought Wilbur a small amount of time.

Finally, his gaze landed on a drawing above the dresser... it was of himself. He studied it for a minute, until an idea came to him. He reached up and took the corner gently in his mouth, and removed it from the wall. Carefully, he carried it in his front teeth and turned back down the hall. He took a glance at the man who was in a daze and slowly getting up. He had to find Ernest before time ran out. As he began to sprint a sharp pain went through his leg. He cried out. The man had caught up, and he had a hold on Wilbur's back leg. Every instinct in him wanted to turn and bite, but he couldn't let go of the drawing. The man got himself up fully and switched his grip to Wilbur's scruff.

"Let's go dog... I can't have you stealing my thunder." Wilbur saw him grab a piece of rope from the curtain ties. He wrapped it tight around Wilbur's neck. "Come on dog... get that stupid drawing out of your mouth as well. Think your smart huh?" The man reached down to take the drawing and Wilbur growled. The man's hand recoiled quickly. "Fine... But you're coming with me." He dragged Wilbur mercilessly through the doors of the inn. Wilbur tried to pull back and fight but the man was strong and the rope was too tight, it burned his neck with every tug.

"I'm taking you back to the forest, and you'd better stay there... Can't have anybody recognizing you either." The man took off his jacket and threw it over Wilbur before continuing to drag him through shady back lanes. Wilbur's heart was heavy. He felt so helpless. His one chance to reunite with Ernest was escaping with every hour. He had to do something. As the man tried to navigate a large puddle in their way, Wilbur slowly dropped the drawing from his mouth. He bared his teeth, and just as he went to bite, there was a flash of white light and a passerby locked eyes with him from underneath the large jacket.

"Hey! Stop!" The stranger shouted.

The horrible man begrudgingly turned to face the stranger.

"Charles?! What on Earth are you doing here? Where are you taking that dog?" The stranger continued.

"None of your business Ben, on either account." Charles gave Wilbur another yank as he tried to move them along. Wilbur put the brakes on as best he could. He liked the look of Ben. He had a very loving face.

"It is most definitely my business. Were you planning to see Maeve while you were here? Sure doesn't look like it... I don't think you realize how hard she works. You left that poor girl in the dust." Ben shook his head in disbelief and mumbled as he shuffled his things about, he replaced his camera into a large leather satchel around his shoulder.

"Of course I was! My little darling girl." His voice was thick and had as much sentiment as a piece of gravel. "Wait what are you doing with that camera? Have you taken my photo?" Charles started to get flustered again.

Wilbur saw Ben roll his eyes."Why are you really here Charles? And uncover that dog please. Or I'll do it."

"If you must know, I'll be running for mayor of Asphodel this autumn." He flashed a seedy proud look. "Now please hand over that camera..." Charles forcefully reached for the satchel. Ben let out a guffaw that surprised everyone including himself. He quickly moved the satchel to his other side. Charles turned beet red.

"How dare you! You better watch yourself Ben. I can and will have that little shop of yours closed down."

Ben rolled his eyes once more and quickly reached down to pull the coat from Wilbur. His gaze changing all at once. "Blinkin heck..." Ben's eyes lit up, he then spotted the drawing on the ground. His eyes darted from the paper to Wilbur as he put the pieces together.

"Goodbye Ben..." Charles gave Wilbur a harsh tug, and an involuntary whimper escaped.

"Unhand him Charles. This is ridiculous. He just wants his friend back. He wants to go home." Ben's face started to harden with anger.

"Absolutely not." He tugged Wilbur one more time. Wilbur's patience snapped like a thread, he lunged forward and his teeth sunk into flesh. He was careful not to draw blood.

"Ahhhh!!! Blasted thing!" Screamed Charles.

Wilbur saw Ben let out a chuckle as the rope went flying. He quickly ran over to Ben with his tail wagging.

"You'll pay for this, both of you. When I'm mayor of this town. I can have that dog put down! Just a snap of my fingers. You hear that mutt?!" He walked off in a furious huff. Ben just laughed as he knelt down to properly greet Wilbur.

"It's you! Bloody hell it's you!" Ben shook his head in disbelief as he stared into Wilbur's eyes. He stroked Wilbur on the head and back. Wilbur felt warm, it felt nice to be in good company again. He wagged his tail and kissed Ben's face over and over. He saw Ben's smile widen as his round cheeks became rosey. "You're not hurt are you? That man is a piece of work. Always has been."

Wilbur stood still for Ben to check him over. He gently removed the rope from Wilbur's neck.

"It's okay lad, my name is Ben and I know your Ernest. He will be very glad indeed to see you." His voice was like warm honey and rain.

Wilbur heard Ernest's name, and a flood of excitement washed over him. He pricked his ears up, and his tail began to wag incessantly, but a concerned look quickly came over Ben as he stared at Wilbur's hind leg. Wilbur looked back too. A small spot on his hind foot had become transparent. "What on Earth?" Ben scratched his chin in dismay.

Wilbur quickly hid his leg and lowered his head. He could see Ben pondering the impossible. He saw his eyes dart from Wilbur to the leg and then to the forest. He went pale as his blue eyes, now glazing over, remained locked to Wilbur's.

"So the myths are true... You're.... no... "

Wilbur cowered along the ground toward Ben's legs. He couldn't bare to look at him anymore.

"Oh, Wilbur... This is bad. Here..." Ben reached into his pocket and pulled out his handkerchief. Wilbur extended his leg to let him wrap it.

"Right... That'll do for now. We cannot tell Ernest. Not until it's time. How much time do you have anyways?" Wilbur looked toward the sun that was now one quarter of the way down towards the horizon.

"Until sundown... right. Should've known. Let's go. Make the most of it alright?" Ben looked at him with stormy eyes, and gave him a gentle pat. "Just come along with me and we'll get you sorted. I know just where they are, or at least where they should be." Ben scooped up the slightly soggy drawing and patted his thigh for Wilbur to follow. "Alright, come on then Wilbur."

Wilbur obliged. As they walked, a black cat began to follow. Wilbur's eyes darted towards him, the cat returned his gaze with a gentle nod. It was now or never.

Chapter Eighteen

Ernest patiently stood at the door with the picnic basket and watched as Maeve frantically ran about the cottage. They had checked three times that they'd gotten everything, but she insisted on checking once more. He discreetly glanced at his watch. He breathed a small sigh of relief realizing they still had plenty of time before the peak of the equinox. The intensity of the day was tangible, but at this moment Ernest felt calm. He knew that Wilbur would show. He could feel it. Maeve bustled out through the door nearly knocking Ernest back. She apologized and quickly fixed the loose pin in her hair. With a smile, she smoothed down her iris blue dress.

"Right, I am convinced we have not left anything behind." She finally declared contentedly.

"Well I am certainly glad for that, fourth time is the charm as they say... We were meant to leave hours ago." Ernest smirked at her, and grabbed her hand. She received him with a dignified huff. Ernest started to feel the butterflies rising up in his stomach as they approached the little gate at the edge of the front garden. He glanced at Maeve, she squeezed his hand and gave him a confident nod. With that, they set out for the yew tree at the edge of the misty forest.

"I really appreciate all you've done Maeve. I've got a good feeling about today." As he said the words, daydreams fluttered like sweet butterflies through his mind. Wilbur back at his side again, day and night. His best friend, his rock, his warmth on the coldest nights. To finally have him back, he had never wanted something so badly. His bones felt like they could jump from his skin.

"I feel it too." She gave Ernest a smile, her eyes huge and hopeful, yet slightly guarded. Her nose scrunched until the bridge met a worried brow, but she seemed to shake it off. She recovered herself in a playful tone. "If he doesn't, I may be very offended that he doesn't like my cooking."

"He'd be a fool Maeve, and a fool he is not!" He gave her an endearing smile, and her face relaxed. "Have you had any more dreams about him lately?"

The hardened expression came back. "Unfortunately not, there were some about Pendle and a few about a strange little rabbit but Wilbur has been absent..."

"Does that mean anything?" Ernest felt his confidence drop slightly.

She hesitated. "I don't think so, my dreams don't always have significance." She tried to sound reassuring.

After a warm walk, they arrived at the scene. The ancient yew tree stood as tall and winding as ever. It looked like something from a fairytale book. Its silhouette sitting just in front of the dark forest. Ernest stared in awe at the enormous being. Eventually he tore his gaze from the tree and slowly handed Maeve the picnic basket. He helped her lay out a large yellow and white gingham blanket. They chose a spot directly in view of the balmy sunlight. Maeve immediately started to busy herself. She set up the different treats in a lovely arrangement, and admired her work.

Ernest left her and started to walk in the opposite direction. He felt oddly drawn to the tree. There was a strange pull. He needed to investigate it further. As he approached, he placed a hand gently upon its gnarled bark. Tracing his fingers over the dent he'd made, he felt some sort of energy. His long fingers began to tingle. His face skewed into perplexity. He removed his hand and stared at it. There was nothing there. He felt foolish as he waited, as if he expected something to happen, but there was only the breeze. Ernest shook his head and decided he'd chalk it all down as nerves. He went to take a step back, but his feet held him in place.

"You okay?!" Maeve called out.

Ernest quickly snapped out of his strange moment. "Yes, sorry! This tree brings back a lot of memories, that's all. It feels so odd standing here again." He called back to her, his eyes only coming away from the tree for a small moment. Maeve just nodded as if she understood. After what felt like hours of contemplation, he willed his feet to move and made his way back over to the blanket. "This looks lovely." He made sure to admire all their hard work. Maeve beamed. "Am I allowed to steal a few bits?" He reached down to grab a bacon roll.

"Not too many now, we may have quite a few hours to wait." She tried to sound strict, before shyly reaching overt to grab a strawberry scone for herself. "Tea?" She asked.

Ernest barely heard her as he fixated on the street behind her head. A gorgeous border collie came over the horizon, but he was following closely behind an older man. Ernest's heart started to beat at a nervous pace once again.

"Ernest... tea?" Maeve asked again.

"Oh, I'm sorry. Yes please. I do apologize. It's just I thought I saw Wilbur, but it couldn't be... I don't think anyway... it looks like he's following an elderly man." He pointed behind her.

Maeve poured the tea and craned her neck back to see. She squinted and placed a hand over her eyes to shield the sun. A gasp quickly followed. "That's Uncle Ben! Ernest, I think that's Wilbur! It has to be!"

Ernest was in a stunned silence. His vision shrunk to telescope size, as he tried to remember to breathe.

Chapter Nineteen

Pendle veered off the path and made himself comfortable on a sunny stone wall near the forest. He watched his master lead Wilbur down the cobbled street. He felt as though his work was almost complete. Even though the circumstances felt less than ideal, he felt like he had done the right thing. His only hope was that Wilbur and Ernest could make peace with what had passed. He closed his green eyes and faced the sun with a deep inhale.

"Ahem... we need to speak with you." Pendle jumped out of his skin, arching his back. He spun on his toes to see Leer peering from the edge of the dark mossy forest. A rustle from the tree above let him know that Rell was also present. Pendle relaxed his posture and nodded, rolling his eyes. He gingerly leapt from the stone wall and disappeared under the cover of the massive trees.

"Please sit..." Leer said in his druid like voice. Rell created a huge gust of wind as he silently floated down to take his spot near the old fox. Pendle dramatically stretched and then did as he was told. Leer cleared his throat once more. "Pendle my dear, we have been well aware of your friend's presence since he arrived in this forest."

"Friend is a bit of an overstatement if you're talking about the dog." He chided.

Leer just shook his head and Rell peered through him with his one good eye. That eye never failed to give Pendle a shutter, it pierced his soul.

The fox continued on. "Yes well, this is beside the point. Wilbur has made some waves here. He is quite the helpful sort. We have seen that he seems to be drawn to the lost ones. We haven't had a soul runner in ages, and the amount of lost ones is ever piling up, and the appearance of the... you know." His powerful voice gave way to a worried tone. "Wisp." He whispered.

"You don't mean?" Pendle stood up and his tail began to twitch. Rell fluffed his feathers out and rotated his head even further towards him. Pendle tried hard not to let it disturb him.

"We have chosen." The owl's voice boomed along the rocks.

Pendle crouched backward, his fur bristled. Leer stood now and approached him sympathetically.

"I thought I was being considered..." Pendle's gaze met the dark forest floor as he spoke.

"I... well we... the council, think you are much better suited to your position as a messenger. You slip through worlds unnoticed, and ahem... the... um... thing doesn't seem to notice you either. This is your gift." Leer tried his best to sound complimentary. Pendle's ears flattened as he abruptly turned away and started to walk out of the forest.

Rell's wings beat the air and his thunderous voice followed. A combination only equivalent to the stormy northern sea. "You will train him Pendle. He will need your guidance. It has been decided. The council is not crossed."

The voice reverberated and followed him closely. Pendle paused, he could feel an eerie hush as the owl disappeared like a specter. He could sense that Leer was still there, he knew the old fox was debating on whether to say anything more. Pendle only heard him turn and go, he imagined him shaking his weary head. No other sound dared slip through the silence. Pendle took a deep breath and closed his eyes tightly. He walked out of the forest into the sun once again. The fog started to creep slowly from the Earth. It reached for his ankles as he made his exit. "I hate dogs."

CHAPTER TWENTY

Ernest was aware that his legs had turned to jelly as he tried to stay upright. Wilbur who had left Uncle Ben's side as soon as their eyes met, was now bounding straight for him. He was so overcome with emotion that he couldn't move a centimeter in any direction, and he felt Maeve place a steadying hand against his back. There was his best friend, running full tilt in his direction. The moment he had longed for. It seemed almost too good to be true, and he could not will his body to listen to him. His eyes welled with tears and his heart felt like it might just stop altogether. Before he could fully register what was happening, his knees buckled under him. Wilbur hadn't been able to stop himself, and they both tumbled to the ground in a heap of fluff and scones.

Ernest opened his eyes to see Wilbur standing over him thoroughly licking his face. Maeve was at the corner of the blanket bent over in a fit of giggles. Happy tears streamed down her cheeks. Ernest just lay there for a minute, embracing the utter bliss of the moment. The sun felt serenely warm, the air luxuriously sweet, and every sound was music. The anxious days of the unknown had come to an end. Finally, he sat up and grabbed Wilbur's fluffy face in his hands. He gently rubbed his silky crooked ears. He held Wilbur's head against his for a long while and closed his eyes. He breathed in deeply, Wilbur's scent alone quieted his soul.

"My sweet boy... it really is you... it really is." He gripped him tighter, afraid of what would happen if he slipped away. Ernest felt tears trickle down his cheeks. All at once there was release and there was relief. He stole a glance at Maeve who sat patiently, her eyes filled to the brim with love. Slowly, he released Wilbur who excitedly turned and sniffed his surroundings, making a curious beeline for Maeve.

"Hello there Wilbur, I've been so looking forward to meeting you." She reached out a hand and gently stroked Wilbur's head. He sniffed her eagerly, his tail wagged incessantly. He placed his gentle head on her shoulder and she gave him a light hug, and closed her eyes. A few tears danced down her rosey cheeks. Ernest knew she was just as happy as he was. Wilbur was well and truly there, finally. "He's so lovely Ernest." She said softly, releasing Wilbur from her grasp. Wilbur turned and gave a look full of pride.

Ernest just smiled and nodded at her silently. A glint of silken blue fabric caught his eye and he noticed the handkerchief around Wilbur's leg. He looked over at Uncle Ben who had been politely standing off to the side. "Come on over Ben, join us won't you?" The sweet old man politely smiled, and finally made his way over. "Do you know what happened to Wilbur's leg? Is it bad?" Ernest asked as Ben slowly groaned and sat with a thump onto the blanket. He clutched at his back with a small wince, but smiled all the while. "Are you alright?" Ernest asked, and reached out a hand.

"Oh fine, just a bit older than I remember most days!" He laughed, and brushed the helpful hand away.

Ernest nodded. "Thank you for bringing him here, I really can't believe this is real. I thought this day would never come."

"Of course boy, as soon as I saw him I knew!" He reached over and gave Wilbur a scratch. "He's just lovely really, and the leg is nothing. Just a little gash. Should heal up." Ben said swiftly.

"That's good to hear. I'll take a look at it later. He is pretty great isn't he?" He beamed at Wilbur who was busy investigating everything and everyone. "I found him on a Welsh farm years ago. Just a little bumbling pup. Cutest little thing." He shook his head lovingly, as the memories flooded in. All four were silent as the sun wrapped them in golden warmth. They watched as Wilbur rolled himself all over the grass in contented bliss. After his romp, he came back to Ernest who was sat in a crisscross position and he knew exactly what his friend wanted. Wilbur quickly circled around and fit himself directly in the middle of Ernest's crossed legs. He leaned his head out onto the blanket and slept as tranquil as ever. Ernest gently ran his fingers down Wilbur's sleek back. They all chatted for some time as Wilbur safely snoozed.

"Ben, I meant to ask, where did you run into Wilbur?" Ernest asked as he fingered Wilbur's velveteen ears.

"Bit of a long story that... Firstly, Maeve your dad is here." He said with a grimace.

Maeve shot him a look of shock. "What?!

"Mhhmm... Ran into him dragging poor Wilbur out of town. Said he's planning to run for mayor... guessing he didn't want somebody or some dog taking away his spotlight. You know how he is."

Ernest felt himself turn red with anger. "He was dragging Wilbur out of town?!"

"Yep, had a tight rope round his neck. I stopped them as soon as I noticed, I did. Saw Wilbur's little face underneath a coat. Charles must have thrown it on him." Ben shook his head in disgust. Maeve was sat in silent outrage.

"Thank god for you Ben...poor boy." He looked sadly down at Wilbur and gently felt around his neck. "That's despicable. I'm sorry Maeve, but..."

"No, you're right.. He's always been the same. I'm sorry he did that to Wilbur." Her eyes had turned to fire in the reflection of the setting sun, steaming tears welled up behind them. Ernest reached a hand over and placed it comfortingly upon her knee. He'd never seen her so upset.

"Do you think he's the one who's tearing down all the posters?" Ernest thought out loud.

"Without a doubt... It has to be. I didn't know he was here. I feel so stupid." She blinked and quickly wiped away her angry tears. She placed her hand on top of Ernest's.

"It's alright Maeve, Wilbur is here now. That's all that matters." Ernest gave her hand a tight squeeze.

"He will not run for mayor. I will do everything in my power." She said fiercely.

"Oh don't worry Maevey, he wont." Ben gave a sly smile as he gestured to his camera bag. "We will just say being a hobby photographer and owning a print shop is quite handy. I could stop him from being anything but a sewer rat with what I've got on him." The smile grew wide and toothy across his face. Maeve smiled knowingly in return and wiped her nose with her handkerchief. Ben reached into his coat pocket and pulled out his tarnished round glasses along with the drawing which he handed over to Ernest. He reached over and quickly ate half of a scone. "He is one smart boy Ernest. He had that in his mouth." Ben gave a slight chuckle of astonishment, his words muffled through the strawberry pastry.

Ernest grabbed the paper and stared at it."Blimey... He's even more clever than I gave hime credit for." He looked down at Wilbur again and gave him a big pat.

"I bet he thought you were at the inn Ernest, I'm sure he traced your scent. You'd only just cleared your stuff out yesterday." Maeve chimed in, her voice started to calm.

"That does make sense. I'm just so glad he made it back. It still doesn't feel real. Something about it just feels so strange, but I don't know what." He scratched his head.

"Everything is fine Ern, you've just been through a lot." Maeve gave him a reassuring look as she laid down on the blanket. She took deep and steadied breaths until her eyes started to flutter closed.

"Enjoy every moment, Ernest." Ben said in an almost sorrowful tone.

The evening was slowly creeping up the horizon as Wilbur sleepily stood and stretched. He gave Ernest another big kiss on his cheek. Ernests's heart felt so full. Maeve was fast asleep on the blanket, and then Uncle Ben slowly stood up as well. A worried look broke over his face, it was desperate. Like he was trying to hold something in. "Has he eaten any of these treats at all?" Ben looked sheepish, almost like he meant to say something else altogether.

Ernest felt small pangs of anxiety come over him. He realized Wilbur hadn't eaten at all. He stared over at him. Wilbur was now patiently sat next to him at the edge of the blanket. His speckled face suddenly seemed to crease with concern as he turned his gaze and stared down at the grassy floor. "You okay Wilbur? Would you like a treat?" Ernest pulled a bacon slice from one of the buns and held it out. Wilbur put his ears down and politely wagged his tail. He turned his nose away. His soft brown eyes gave Ernest a side-eyed stare. His lopsided ears a charmingly crooked frame, but something wasn't right. "Hmm... are you worried Wilbs? Maybe he's just too excitable right now." He said hopefully, and looked over at Ben expecting him to have a word of guidance. Ben stayed silent. Ernest started to feel uneasy, but he didn't know why. He noticed Maeve start to rouse from her cat nap. Sleepy words breached her lips.

"Are we ready to go home then?" She rubbed her eyes and stretched.

"Yeah, I think that'd be best for everybody." Uncle Ben agreed gently and helped gather the remnants of their picnic. Ernest noticed that he would not make eye contact anymore. He knew something was up. He turned again to his best friend.

"Well come on Wilbur! Let's go! There's been some changes, but you're going to love it! I know you will." Wilbur wagged his tail but did not follow. "Wilbur... Come on, boy. I promise it isn't bad." Ernest coaxed. Wilbur was steadfast. He began to whine and turn his head away."What is going on with you Wilbs? We have to go..." Ernest worriedly turned to Maeve and Ben.

"Come on Wilbur! Come on!" Maeve tried, patting her knees.

Wilbur began to whine heavily. The whines became soft barks, and he remained glued to the ground. The sun was swiftly disappearing. Ernest started to panic. Wilbur never disobeyed. He walked over to him. "Wilbur... you're okay. You have to come along. It's getting dark. Everything will be okay, I promise! Are you feeling alright?" Ernest reached down to try and shove Wilbur along, but he froze in his tracks. Ernest eyed Wilbur's long tail. It was fading into thin air. Ernest felt his face flush pale white.

"Ernest? What's the matter?" Maeve called softly. She made her way over followed by Uncle Ben. They both stopped fast. Wilbur was whimpering as his back legs became translucent. Ernest snapped out of his daze and rushed to the front of Wilbur.

"Wilbur! What the bloody hell is happening?!" He screamed through teary eyes. Wilbur bowed his head and pinned back his ears, he averted his gaze.

"He needs to show you something, Ernest." Ben said somberly as he placed a hand on Ernest's shoulder. Wilbur hunched his back, he cowered towards the tree line. As he neared the forest he turned and began to whimper once more. He sat and he waited there at the trees. Ernest's hands were shaking. Maeve and Ben barely dared to breathe.

"You're right... he wants us to follow him..." Ernest's voice emerged shaky and riddled with nerves. They all silently followed Wilbur into the forest. Eventually, they came upon a grove of wildflowers and trees. Wilbur went up ahead and then stopped once more, he sat. He still refused to look at Ernest. As they all approached him he backed away in a worried posture. Maeve stepped back and grabbed Uncle Ben's arm to keep him in place. Ernest walked closer to his friend who was now faded up to his shoulders. Wilbur looked down to his right and whined, his ears pinned as far back as they could go. He continued to look away as Ernest finally saw why they were there.

Ernest's eyes filled to the brim with warm tears as he gazed upon the real Wilbur, what was left of him. Lying dead in the wildflowers. He collapsed immediately. His face pressed against the corpse of his friend. Heaving sobs echoed through the mighty forest. Roars of despair flew through the balmy evening air. The sound of a heart breaking had never been so loud. Maeve and Uncle Ben sat in the background crying silent tears as they held each other. Wilbur was fading fast, but he approached his best friend. He lay down next to him and curled under his arm. Ernest could barely breathe, he could barely see through his tears. As he sobbed over Wilbur's ghost and his physical body the only words he could seem to utter were "Why?"

"Why Wilbur?" Why?" He uttered a million times over. His sobs becoming more uncontrollable. Wilbur cowered and tried his best to be comforting. Ernest sat up and tightly hugged Wilbur's ghostly face. The only thing that was left. "Please Wilbur... Please don't go." He felt Wilbur nuzzle into him as best as he could. He knew he had to let go. "I love you so much... We will find each other again Wilbur. Do you hear me? Do you hear me?!" Wilbur nodded and mustered one last tender lick onto Ernest's teary face before he faded away completely. Ernest was left grasping at the air. He fell to the ground once more and wept in desperate silence. Maeve and Uncle Ben came over and sat with him. He felt Maeve's comforting touch on his back.

"I'm sorry boy..." came Ben's saddened voice.

"You knew! Ben you knew!" Ernest was felt his blood boiling. As he yelled into the dirt beneath him. "How could you not tell me?!" Ben only looked down. Ernest turned onto his side, and held what remained of one of Wilbur's front paws.

"Ern... would you have enjoyed your evening if you knew?" Ben meekly replied.

Ernest remained in silent tears. He knew Ben did the right thing, but he couldn't accept it. Not any of it.

"Did you know as well Maeve?!" He turned on her.

"How could..."

"Your dreams Maeve! This forest... How long did you know?!" He shot her a look.

Maeve looked crushed and he immediately regretted his words. "Ernest... I will be honest in saying that I had my concerns with dreaming he was in this forest, but I really didn't know he was gone. Not at all. I wouldn't have lead you on. I promise." Her comforting hand pulled away from his back. Ernest propped himself up on his forearms and looked up through his tears. "I know... I'm sorry. I just... I feel so empty but yet there's almost relief. Relief in knowing his fate, but why this Maeve? Why this? We didn't deserve this ending. He didn't deserve this. We didn't deserve this. My boy..." His sobs overtook him again, his face falling onto dirty hands.

"It's normal Ernest... you've just lost your greatest friend. Your only friend for many years. This is one of the hardest things anyone could ever go through... Trust me.. I know." Her voice became soft and forgiving. She laid down next to him and rubbed his back. She held him close. Ben inched closer and continued to look at the ground, but Ernest knew he meant well. Far on into the night, Ernest finally sat up and wiped his dirt-covered face with his sleeve. All he could do was stare blankly into the cold distance. Maeve sat up with him, and held his hand in one of hers, while the other stroked Wilbur's back amongst the tall green grass. Ernest took a deep breath.

"I'd like to bury him... by the yew tree."

CHAPTER
TWENTY-ONE

Pendle's ears sagged and his tail was still. Downcast, he watched everything from atop a branch only a few meters away. The whole scene was horrid, and there was nothing he could do. His ear twitched as a bramble moved in the distance. Two round fluffy rabbits emerged.

"Ah, it's you two again."

Pippin looked down, despondent. "We heard the cries all the way over by our tree."

Violet stared into the distance and wiped away a tear. The daisy behind her ear slowly fell to the ground. She picked it up and held the drooping flower between her tiny paws.

Pendle jumped to the ground silently and walked over to them. "It really is a miserable day."

The rabbits nodded in synch.

"Well, Wilbur will be glad to see you two anyways. He'll need some support. I've had a rather daft meeting with the forest council." He said with a roll of his green eyes.

Pippin pricked up an ear. "Oh? What do you mean?"

Pendle casually groomed a paw. "They want Wilbur to be the new soul runner."

Pippin and Violet's eyes shot open. "I thought you..." Violet began nervously.

"Please... don't. I know. However, I have realized I am better suited to my messenger position. I've had a think. A clumsy old dog certainly couldn't be the messenger." He cooly convinced himself. Again the bunnies nodded in agreement.

Pippin tried to sound encouraging. "You guys'll make a great team I think!" He urged.

Pendle just sighed and continued his grooming. "I guess it will have to do," He said, sounding soft against his will. An eerie shift in the wind came through the trees.

"Is it the wisp?" Violet whispered, her little body shuttered.

"Shhhh, that will be taken care of as well." Pendle said, he sat very still and the bunnies wiggled their noses in the direction of the haunting breeze. Pendle's voice came again in a hurried whisper. "He's coming, shush now. We will tell him about this later. He needs time."

CHAPTER TWENTY-TWO

Wilbur clenched his jaw as he tried to ignore the sound of heart-wrenching cries bursting through the trees. With each step further into that cursed wood, he knew he could not turn back. He could not comfort Ernest anymore. He kept his eyes down and his ears low. The wailing and screaming started to fade away. Mostly, he was glad that the cries of his name had stopped. He hoped that maybe Ernest would just forget about him.

Eventually, he heard small low voices. He recognized them right away. His friends had waited for him. He knew they would try and make him feel better, but Wilbur wasn't sure that he ever could. He would do his best, for them. The rain started to pierce the veil of the treetops above him and it trickled down his nose, as if to mock his own tears. When he reached his friends, his sadness was too heavy to bear. His whole body hit the ground with a thud. He lay there on the cold forest floor as the rain soaked through his speckled fur.

Pippin approached first and snuggled into Wilbur's haunch, but the little rabbit did not say a word. Wilbur was thankful. He had no energy for small condolences. Not now. Violet had disappeared and quickly returned with a small blanket. She heaved it over Wilbur's back. He felt her settle in next to Pippin. Pendle stayed under a bush nearby to keep himself dry, but Wilbur noticed that he kept a thoughtful watch over them.

Wilbur was despondent, but he was very glad to have friends like these. As night drew nearer, Wilbur stood and silently lead the way to the old hollow. The one he and Pippin had stayed in before. He was tired and finally had enough of being soaked through. Leer must've known they were coming. The hollow was warm and lit with candles. There were enough blankets for everyone. Wilbur went in first and settled down at the back. The bunnies followed and cozied up in a blanket. Pendle stayed near the opening.

"I must be going home dear Wilbur, but it looks like you have some support." He gave a small smile at the two sleeping rabbits on either side. "I truly am sorry. These things are never easy, but you've done well. I must add that there are some things we must discuss, whenever it is you feel ready of course." His voice broke the night as nonchalant as ever, but his body language said what he did not. Wilbur just nodded at Pendle. He still could not bring himself to speak a single word. Pendle's warm green eyes gave way to genuine sympathy. His tail flicked slowly.

"Okay then, goodnight to all. I'll come to check in on you in the morning." Pendle blew out the candles one by one and Wilbur watched him disappear into the dark night. He fell asleep quickly and from the silence he assumed Violet and Pippin did as well.

"Hello?! Hello?!" A strange voice echoed through the hollow from afar. Wilbur's ears twitched and he opened one sleepy brown eye. "Is there anybody here? What is this? Am I dead?! Somebody please help!"

The voice was shaken, but somehow light in its tone. Wilbur slowly got to his feet, careful not to wake the bunnies. He peered into the blinding morning light. At the edge of the wood he could see a man wandering around.

"Hello?! Anyone at all?!"

Wilbur sniffed the air intently. The man looked very familiar. Wilbur looked back to make sure he hadn't woken his friends. His curiosity got the best of him, and he made a stealthy exit. He walked quietly toward the odd man. Keeping his distance, he let out a small "ruff". The man turned on his heels.

"Oh! Well hello, look at you. You surprised me! Are you okay?" The man held out his hand slowly.

Wilbur got closer and immediately recognized him. It was Sam! The soldier he and Ernest had picked up on their last day together. He tried to block the memories from shooting through his head again. He wanted to forget. But how could he?

He stared up intently at Sam, who was quite a handsome man. He gave him some small curious sniffs. He still wore his army green trench coat and trousers. His reddish blonde hair was gently combed to one side, which revealed a large burn on the side of his face. He held a soldier's helmet in his right hand. Wilbur gave his extended hand a quick lick to show he was friendly. Sam gave a warm smile. Wilbur felt overcome with emotion to see a familiar face, and one that Ernest would've known as well.

"Do you think you can help me little friend? I'm not sure what's going on or how I got here, but I'm a bit spooked to tell you the truth." Sam looked around nervously.

Wilbur tilted his head inquisitively hoping that Sam would give some more information.

"Right... well you can't exactly talk so how are we going to do this?... I got it!" Sam took a seat on a large log nearby and stared at Wilbur. "Okay, we can give this a try. Please bark once if you know where we are."

"Ruff!" Wilbur wagged his tail, this was interesting.

"Great! Now… this is an odd one, but I'm just going to come out with it… please bark twice if I'm dead. I know, I sound like a lunatic. But it isn't impossible. Not considering where I've just come from." Sam partially hid his face behind his free hand and waited for the hard truth. Wilbur felt sad for him, but he couldn't lie. He wanted to help, it was in his nature to help. It was the only thing that seemed to make him feel something other than sadness. He knew Ernest would want the same. Ernest would be proud. He also knew now that nothing was impossible.

He gave Sam his honest answer. "Ruff. Ruff." He turned his head away, and waited for a less than happy reaction.

Sam rubbed his forehead and was quiet for a moment. "Right… I had a horrible feeling. The last thing I remember was being in the trenches with my brigade. There was a flash of light, and I don't remember waking up… obviously because I didn't. I can't say I'm too surprised." Sam looked contemplative, as he stared out into the trees, taking it all in. This life after life. Wilbur approached gently and sat near his feet. He put his head on Sam's lap. He understood, better than anyone. He gave a heavy sigh and they both stared out, trying to grasp onto anything that lay beyond the tree filled horizon. Wilbur saw the smile creep back over Sam's face.

"What about you huh? Are you…?" Sam stopped himself, and stroked Wilbur's ears gently. Wilbur felt his heart go heavy, as he sighed once more. "Yeah, I was afraid so. Well, I appreciate you being here for me anyway. I thought I was completely alone. It doesn't feel quite as scary anymore, now you're here. You're a real good dog, and I'm sure somebody is missing you something terrible right now." His small ear rubs turned into full body scratches. Wilbur felt their feelings intermingle. Their energies collided and tussled with each other, and then just for a second, they seemed to settle. His tail gave in to small wags.

Sam spoke again, in a more serious tone. "One more question… my wife Dianna, she died a couple of years ago. She was very sick, and there is not a day that goes by when I don't wish for her. I would do anything to see her again." His brow creased with a heart wrenching look, and his voice cracked. "Is it possible she's here as well? Could you bark once if you might know where I can find her?" The words were barely formed.

Wilbur perked up. He did know. He gave a reassuring bark."Ruff!"

Sam perked up as well. He was astonished. He slowly stood and brushed his hair back with a look of complete disbelief. Wilbur ran in circles. He dipped forward and back and nipped at Sam's pant legs. The sweet soldier's face broke into a huge smile of relief. "Lead the way!" He exclaimed.

As they walked along the winding river, Sam hummed in tune with the song birds. The babble of the river gave them a steady beat. Wilbur liked him. Even in death, he was happy. It was very comforting. The day had become quite warm, and they stopped together every now and then to get a cool drink from the crystal water running alongside of them.

"You sure it's okay to drink this water?" Sam looked down slightly perplexed.

Wilbur just nudged him and gave him a nod.

"Alright, whatever you say. Hey, do we even need to drink anymore? I just thought of that... well I guess it's the sensation isn't it? It's still nice to feel that cold water run through you." Sam took a long contented sip. Wilbur grunted in agreement and they continued on.

"This place is actually quite beautiful. The trees are the greenest I've ever seen. Probably on account of all this mist." Sam looked round in awe as if he were on a different planet.

This place beautiful? Wilbur thought. He took a good look around, and took in a deep breath. This time he tried his best embrace it. This strange world that had turned his own upside down. Up until now, he'd always felt frantic in these woods. He never made time to appreciate them, in fact, he hated them for most of his journey. The mist was his enemy. It took his friends, his life... but he knew deep down that it was not the forest's fault. Sam was right. It was actually quite breathtaking. Some of the trees were hundreds of feet tall, they endlessly reached towards the sky as if asking to be taken home themselves. Their bark was carpeted in the darkest emerald green, an they sparkled in the shy rays of the sun. Their roots were gnarled and spiraling in all directions. It was enchanting, something a rich man might pay a pretty penny to wander through.

But no matter the beauty, he still wished for Ernest. Wished that he was there to walk with them. He would always wish for Ernest. The only thing that quelled his longing was knowing that Ernest was alive and well, and for now the company of Sam, whose deep tender voice broke through Wilbur's thoughts.

"Wow! Look at that! I've never seen a weeping willow that big!" Sam stopped in his tracks. He looked almost star struck.

Wilbur realized they had arrived! "Ruff! Ruff!" Wilbur ran back and forth and wagged his tail.

"Ahh, this is the place huh? Stunning really... where do we go now? Is Dianna here?" He looked around in every direction.

Wilbur took Sam to the base of the tree and sat down. Sam followed suit and sat next to him, using a large root for a backrest. Soon, people started to gather. Not as many as before, but the calling out of names began quickly. Wilbur stood up and cocked his head at Sam.

"Oh! This is it?... how strange. Okay then, this is it! Wait here for me?" He asked, his voice like an excited child. Wilbur nodded. Sam nervously held his helmet and thumbed the straps, he brushed his strawberry blonde hair back, as he built up the courage to join the masses. He quickly disappeared into the swirl of bodies. Wilbur lay back down near the base of the tree. He dreamed of his best friend. Would he ever be able to see him again? Like before? Were there more equinoxes? He needed to speak with Leer again. He scanned the area for the ancient fox, but there was no sign. He decided to try and nap, he liked to see Ernest when he closed his eyes. Slowly, he began to doze, until he saw Sam run excitedly by. He ran straight into the arms of an elegant woman. They hugged and kissed for a long time. The woman held Sam's face in her delicate hands. She traced her thumb over the burn. Both of them could barely speak through their tears. Wilbur tried to listen in.

"I actually found you! You're here... next to me again. How? How is any of this possible?" Sam shook his head. "You know what, I'll take it. I don't even care how." His face fixed into a huge smile and his eyes welled up. "I'd rather death together, than a life alone. Without your beautiful face." He traced her face now, slowly and delicately. "You were gone for so long Dianna." Sam's voice was broken. His eyes were glued to her.

"Sam... I... I am truly sorry I had to leave you so soon. It's never what I wanted, not in a million years. Never what I dreamed in a million life times." She kissed his lips once more, as if to make sure he was real. Then, her gaze focused on the burn again. Her face filled with concern. "What on Earth happened to you? I expected to see you again in this world... but not until I could barely recognize you. Weathered from all the decades gone by. It's too early Sam. How did you find me? You fool!" But her smile was undisguisable.

"It may be too early, and we both know I'm a fool, but I couldn't be happier than I am right now, standing here with you. I was never the same after you were gone." His face was overcome with sadness as the horror flashed through his eyes. "I've been at war Dianna, and it is worse than you could ever imagine. So much anger, so much death, and starving and madness. Pure evil." He put his forehead to hers in an attempt to quiet his thoughts. "My regiment was down in the foxholes and one night there was a gigantic flash... horrible blood-curdling screams, and then I never woke up." Tears fell from her as she listened, gently caressing his scars again. He held onto her hand as it moved along his face. He continued. "A dog managed to find me and lead me here to you... I don't know how he did it. How did you know to come here?"

"I didn't, I just hoped, hoped everyday that someday would be the day." She said tenderly.

Sam smiled in disbelief. They were silent as they hugged again and wiped away tears.

They eventually turned from each other, and Wilbur saw Sam peer through the crowd to try and locate him. Finally they locked eyes. Sam smiled and pointed at him, as he and Dianna approached. Wilbur's anxieties dimmed, if only a little, to see what he had done.

"I can't believe it! You were right!" Dianna, she's right here! This is some sort of magic." Sam called to him.

THE UNDERTAKER AND HIS DOG

Wilbur sat up tall as Sam grabbed the woman's hand and twirled her around. Her baby blue dress spinning in the breeze. She was a beautiful dark-haired woman. Her eyes matched the emerald of the trees. Her face was soft and she reminded Wilbur of a swan. Wilbur jumped up and wagged his tail. He ran circles around them and gently licked their hands. Dianna giggled a beautiful little noise. Sam beamed.

"Oh my goodness! This is him? This handsome one right here? Does he need a home? He is just precious. Our little ghost dog." She smiled and crouched to pet him. Wilbur looked proud as he received her praise.

"That's the very one. I actually don't know his name...He has no tags. I just call him a friend." Sam gave him a wink. "He sure knows his way around here. Don't you boy?" Sam knelt down and gave Wilbur a big hug. "You really are a good one." Sam pulled Wilbur in and they rested their foreheads together. Wilbur's heart dropped as his thoughts pulled him back to this same moment with Ernest. Everything felt frozen in time. Dianna joined in, scratching Wilbur's back. Sam stood and wiped a few tears from his cheeks. Dianna soon followed and joined arms with him. It all felt like slow motion. Sam's voice came through like shattered glass.

"You are one of a kind sweet boy. Thank you so much." He squeezed Dianna's arm. "And as for giving you a home with us... it's very tempting... but." He glanced at Dianna's hopeful face. "I guess it doesn't hurt to ask. Would you want to come with us? I'm sure we could find a nice spot for you. A warm fire. It's your decision little friend, I won't force you."

Wilbur thought of joining them, in a warm and cozy cottage. Rain tapping on the window, but with no chance of making its way in. Just the peaceful pitter patter sound. The friendly rubs and pets. The food. He looked up at them, their eager faces looking down at him. Hope filled their phantasmal eyes. He felt his paw start to step toward them against his will. He stopped himself. He couldn't. They were not Ernest, his heart could never settle. It wouldn't be fair to them. He shot a deeply saddened look to Sam who understood immediately.

"No, we couldn't do that to you boy. I know there's somebody very special out there waiting for you." He turned to a slightly disappointed Dianna and gave her another squeeze before he continued. "I sincerely hope you get to see them again, whoever it is. You deserve the world. You are a hero." They both looked down at him with warm smiles and Wilbur felt a dim happiness seep through him again. He wagged his tail as they turned to go. Dianna reached out for one last stroke. They turned back only once more to wave, once they reached the end of the willow. A ghostly figure hovered over them, and shrieked itself away, as they walked on into the mist disappearing in an instant. They were fulfilled. The happiness continued to creep through Wilbur and he wasn't sure how long it would last.

The realization came over him that he had helped various souls crossover, and it was hard to believe. No matter how sad he was, this feeling nagged at him. They always seemed to find him. Could this be his calling? Was he some sort of spirit guide? Was this his fate? His purpose? Maybe somehow this is the way he could be with Ernest again. But how? He sat and thought for a while as the billowy fog closed in on him. Maybe he needed to talk to somebody.

He remembered that he'd left Pippin and Violet behind, and decided to make a start back to the hollow. They were probably worried about him. He turned back toward the willow and started to make his way. Suddenly, the sound of hushed wing beats fell around him. Seconds later, Rell landed himself on a nearby stump. The large owl stared at him pridefully. Leer and Pendle quietly stepped from behind the ancient willow. They sat in a row silently, watching him carefully as he unsurely looked around.

"Please Wilbur, have a seat. I know you've been through hell, but there is much to tell you. Welcome to the other side of Asphodel."

Chapter Twenty-Three

In the looming sun of early dawn, Ernest trailed slowly behind Maeve and Uncle Ben. Wilbur's fragile body was nestled in his arms. In a somber procession they made their way to the yew tree. He wanted to give Wilbur a proper burial. Ernest looked up to the sky trying to keep more tears from rolling down. Every few steps Maeve turned to give him a comforting smile, but a sadness shrouded her warm eyes. As they got within reaching distance of the old yew, Ernest carefully laid Wilbur down and began to dig at the base of its roots. Maeve sat in the tall grass and weaved a small wreath of willow branches and bluebells, and Uncle Ben read a few bits of tender poetry. It helped cover the deafening silence.

Ernest wiped the sweat from his brow over and over as the sun climbed higher into the midday sky. On the last thrust of his shovel, Ernest struck something. He peered down into the hole and saw a giant root deep in the soil. It glowed from the inside with vibrant ambers and yellows. He did a double-take. With eyes wide, he climbed partially into the hole and traced his fingers along the root. White light burst from the gash his shovel had left. Ernest stood back and stared in disbelief.

"Ernest, you okay down there?" Maeve called.

Ernest couldn't form words. He could hear footsteps getting closer and closer, but he was frozen. As soon as Maeve peered into the hole the light disappeared. He could only continue to stare at it, dumbfounded. He leaned on his shovel and scratched his head.

"Ernest? Everything alright?" Maeve called down to him again.

"Oh uh... yeah, thought I'd found something down here, just an old root." He turned and clambered out of the dirt. Maeve reached out a quick hand to help. She looked at him inquisitively.

"You look like you've seen a ghost..." Maeve said softly.

Ernest gently tossed the shovel aside and gazed back toward the hole and then to the treeline.

"Oh I'm sorry Ern, I didn't mean to..."

"No, no. It's okay. I'm just tired I think." He said rubbing his eyes. His hands left dirt marks across his cheeks. Maeve reached out and he felt a gentle hand massage his shoulder.

"Everything okay over there?" Uncle Ben called out.

"Yeah, nothing to worry about." Ernest replied with a politely dismissive wave. Ben nodded and went back to lying on the grass, he covered his face with his poetry book to block the sun.

Ernest stood silently for a good few minutes. He took a few deep and shaky breaths. This wouldn't be easy, but it was all he could do. He looked out to the treeline one last time, and then back at the magical yew tree. In a hesitant breath he said "Right, I think it's time." He turned around and very delicately gathered Wilbur's body in his arms for what would be the very last time. Maeve stood back, but within reach. Uncle Ben slowly got up and came over, he stood carefully to the side. As Ernest laid his friend to rest, the world went quiet.

The trees stopped their sway, and the bees paused their frantic buzzing. There was only the gentle beat of a butterfly's wing. Mouse-like sniffles from Maeve broke the silence. She went to stand near Uncle Ben who offered a comforting arm. Ernest looked down at his best friend. He bent down and gave his speckled face one final touch. A single tear trickled down and splashed against Wilbur's cheek. Ernest slowly backed himself out of the hole and began covering Wilbur with a soft blanket of dirt. After he finished, he sat there quietly for a long time. Maeve eventually came and placed her floral wreath over the grave. It was the perfect touch, woven with love and a glimmer of life. After many quiet moments, Ernest finally took Maeve's hand and stood.

"It's been me and Wilbur for as long as I can remember... An undertaker and his dog. Until this moment, it never occurred to me that one day I'd have to bury my best friend as well."

Uncle Ben and Maeve stood by his side, as they each offered gentle touches of consolation. Ernest couldn't help but feel like this wasn't the end. Maybe it was just denial. He forced out a few last words.

"Goodbye, Wilbs. I will see you again someday. I know I will. It's you and me forever." He couldn't leave it at anything other than that. Whether he was in denial or not, a final goodbye was too bleak for his heart to handle.

"Let's go get some rest," Maeve whispered. She firmly grabbed Ernest's hand in hers. Ernest nodded. Uncle Ben turned and led the way. After some time Ernest spoke again.

"I think it might be to time for me to call James. I've been putting it off.. I didn't want anymore sadness, but he deserves ti know."

"Did he know Wilbur very well?" Maeve asked, tucking her hair behind one ear as they walked. The quiet of the old cobbled streets started to give way. The morning bustle began with shy whispers and apologies.

Ernest tried his best to return them with thoughtful smiles.

"Well yes and no. I think he will be sad for me mostly, and then I have to tell him that I'm leaving the job as well." Ernest felt his heart race again. He'd almost forgotten that he had decided to rearrange his life with Wilbur. Briefly, he wondered if it was still the right decision. He looked over at Maeve and Ben. They'd never given up. Not once. His old home, his old life, none of it existed without Wilbur.

"Did you want to work in the graveyard here? With Lou?" Ben asked.

"Lou? Is that who owns it? Do you know him?" Ernest asked somewhat hopefully.

"Of course I know Lou! We go way back. Our wives were the best of friends. He'll take you on with no problem, no questions asked. He's been telling me he needs help over there. Not sure exactly what he'd have ya do, but something always needs doing." He smiled in his usual way. He had a way about him that made Ernest feel like things would be okay. He understood why Maeve was so fond of him. His smile was full of warmth and optimism.

A dim light came into Ernest's face. "That's really great news! I could try to see him tomorrow. If you think that would be okay."

"Oh aye, he's a lovely man. He does have a hearse there as well. Doesn't do many pickups, think he's scared to drive. Maybe he'd let you take that on."

"That would be perfect. I definitely know my way around a hearse. It'll be hard without Wilbur, but... I'd like to give it a shot again." Ernest felt a squeeze on his hand from Maeve.

"Just don't overextend yourself. Take your time Ernest." She squeezed his hand again and gave him a knowing smile.

Ernest replied with an understanding nod.

"Good luck boy, I'll drop by and let him know you're keen to come around. Like Maeve said... take your time." He patted Ernest's shoulder. "I must be going now I'm afraid, this is where I split off." Ernest and Maeve paused to say goodbye. Ben moved to shake Ernest's hand and pulled him in for a tender hug. He whispered to him. "You'll be okay Ern, we'll get you sorted. Me and Maevey will take good care of you. Wilbur too." He pulled away and gave Ernest a friendly wink. Ernest replied with a nod and a teary smile. Ben stepped off and leisurely walked down the street with a wave. "Oh one more thing Maevey! You need to drop by my print shop tomorrow... We have a different sort of poster to make." Uncle Ben and Maeve exchanged knowing glances. They all waved once more and headed their separate ways. Ernest grabbed hold of Maeve's hand again as they made their way to the cottage.

"It'll be okay Ern... I'm always here. We can do solstice picnics every year if you'd like? If we make it a tradition... you're bound to see Wilbur again. Especially now that he knows where we'll be. Even in death, he's one smart dog." She was trying her best.

Ernest squeezed her hand and smiled. He admired her unending optimism. "Yeah, I'd like that actually. Anything is worth trying. I just wish it was more than a few times a year. This is all just very surreal." His voice became weak again, almost hollow. He gave her a small peck on the cheek, and hoped her rosiness would bring some color back to him. He saw her blush and fumble with the latch on the gate. He smiled, and it did make him feel a bit more vibrant. As soon as they were in the door, Maeve began making tea. Ernest sat in silence on the warm floral patterned sofa. He stared through the wall as he recalled the otherworldly events that had led him to that moment. If someone wrote a story about it, nobody would believe it. But he knew, no matter what, he was glad to have friends like these. He would see his Wilbur again... someday.

A harsh knock at the front door caused Ernest to surface from deep within his thoughts. He cautiously got up to answer it. As he opened the door a large man with slicked hair stood tall in the doorframe. He was as wide as the doorway itself. His eyes were intensely blue. He flashed Ernest a wide grin. It made his skin crawl. It was the man he'd seen on the steps of the inn.

"Hello there lad... who are you? Is Maeve here?" His voice was like slime, slippery and unpredictable.

"I should ask you the same... who are you?" Ernest straightened his shoulders and tried to appear larger.

"I'm Charles lad... call me Charlie if you want. You know who I am... everyone does. Maevey would've told you her dad was in town surely." He smirked.

"I won't be calling you anything, and she sure didn't... you're the one who was dragging my dog around town." Ernest aggressively inched closer. Charles uncomfortably tried looking around him to spot Maeve. "She's not here." Ernest lied.

"Well tell her I'd like to see her, and yes I do apologize for that. How is your little guy doing? Did you manage to get him back?" His tongue rolled gingerly off the roof of his mouth trying its best to replicate sympathy.

"I've just buried him... thanks for your concern." He said through cold teeth.

"Oh how terribly sad, when I'm mayor we can sort a proper dog out for you I'm sure." He flashed another grin. Ernest formed his hands into tight fists. He could feel his ears turn blood red. It took everything to restrain himself. He raised one hand and slammed the door hard in Charles' face, or possibly onto his face, but either way he wasn't bothered. As he took a deep breath Maeve came in from the back garden.

"Ern... are you okay? Was somebody here?" Her voice was like a sweet melody compared to the filth that had just crawled through his ears.

"Nobody... make sure you go down to the print shop tomorrow. I have a feeling it's going to be really important." His teeth were still clenched. He went and sat down on the sofa again. He stared blankly. Maeve looked at him concerned, raising an eyebrow.

"I'll finish up that nice cup of tea for you." She said, as she wiped her hands on her pinny and disappeared back into the kitchen. Ernest pulled out the soggy drawing of Wilbur and spread it onto the table. His hard expression melted into something a bit softer, and became softer still as the sound of Maeve humming over the kettle drifted into the sitting room.

Chapter Twenty-Four

Wilbur sat, the forest floor cold on his paws. He faced the panel and waited for them to continue. His heart beat quickly. Rell's booming voice came first.

"Wilbur, we are of course aware of the tragedy that has befallen you and even moreso the fresh loss of your best friend. For this, we are deeply sorry. Please accept our sincerest condolences." He stared at Wilbur sat there all alone, and the sadness was apparent in his one-eyed gaze. "However, we have noticed you've shown a certain prowess during your time here. You seem to jump at the chance to help the lost ones, and it seems to fulfill you if only briefly. We can see that you have been deeply content in the help you give others and you have even managed to leave this forest and see your best friend again... but yet your soul still has not dispersed from this wood. You are still not entirely fulfilled, which leads us to believe you are special."

Wilbur was intrigued. He tilted his head inquisitively. Leer spoke next. The ancient fox stood and walked closer to him. "You are a soul runner Wilbur..." The godlike fox smiled with a thousand friendly teeth.

"I'm sorry... a what?" Wilbur was taken aback.

Pendle impatiently chimed in. "Ugh dogs... you run souls. You guide them through the forest until they are fulfilled and can reach their true afterlives." His tail flicked back and forth.

Wilbur was stunned. "I... I can't believe this. Are you sure?" He shuffled his paws nervously.

"Yes my dear child, you have been chosen. We haven't had a soul runner in ages. The accumulation of lost souls has gotten out of hand for us. We can only do so much.... And then there's the uh.., wisp. A whole myriad of problems really." The old owl shook his head in dismay.

"I... I don't know what to say. I'm honored... but what does this mean? And what could I possibly do about the... wisp."

Pendle rolled his green eyes. "It only means that you continue on with the official title. You patrol the edges of the forest each day and see who needs help, and you keep the *wisp* away, but really if there is a soul runner in place the floating bat brain keeps to itself. You've already been doing it Wilbur." Rell gave Pendle a light smack with the edge of his wing. Pendle jumped and a sharp hiss escaped.

"Do not pay him any mind. You will continue as the great soul runner and you will be doing us a great service. What do you say?" Rell's voice echoed along the trees with pride. "And you will get a soul messenger to help navigate between worlds, this is where Pendle comes in for you." Pendle looked over at Wilbur and gave a sarcastic bow.

"You may also choose a forest navigator. Should you need help finding your way." Leer added warmly.

Wilbur was quiet as he took it all in. He looked over at Pendle who didn't offered a slightly encouraging glance. "I really am honored... I suppose if I have to be here for an eternity I might as well make myself useful... especially with something that I enjoy doing. I do truly enjoy it, you're right about that." He thought out loud. He shifted his weight back and forth as he mulled it over. His caramel expression melted into a look of deep concern. "Will I still be able to see Ernest? When the veil thins?"

Everyone fell silent. Wilbur became increasingly worried as the silence lingered. He looked over at Pendle whose ears were now back. Wilbur looked down at the dirt.

"My dear boy, as a soul runner... you may only leave here if it is on important business. You cannot leave for leisure. It just isn't done." Leer said sadly, he approached Wilbur and put an ancient paw onto one of his own. His eyes were gentle, like a homely familiar fire. His face hoary, but timeless. "We must also tell you that whomever you pick as your forest navigator... will fall under the same jurisdiction. They can never leave... never truly move on."

"Pippin..." Wilbur whispered as a tear began to form. The old owl and the strange cat approached gently. "What if I say no?" Wilbur asked nervously.

"Then eventually... you become one of the lost ones... never being fulfilled. You'll no longer remember your old life. It will be erased slowly and surely." Pendle said, his voice had softened. His hard exterior once again gave way, as he saw that Wilbur was truly struggling. He placed his small head on Wilbur's chest and purred softly. Wilbur breathed deeply. The smells of the forest wafted through him. He smelled the sadness and the desperation of all those who needed him. A montage of memories flooded his mind.

He and Ernest. Their whole lives together like a warm and familiar movie. His home. If he said no... It would all be gone. Fade like nothing but a silly dream. He couldn't let the happen. He couldn't bring himself to lose those memories... it was one thing not to be with Ernest physically... but he could never risk losing him entirely. His gaze floated to the treeline. A shadow caught his eye. Pippin and Violet were hiding shyly behind a small tree. He knew they'd heard everything. Violet clung to her big brother who seemed to look stronger than he ever had. The little rabbit tried his best to puff out his chest. He stood tall and gave Wilbur a confident nod.

Everything rushed through Wilbur's head at once, and in one deep breath Wilbur spoke. "I'll do it... I'll become your soul runner."

Chapter Twenty-Five

Maeve awoke early the next morning. She quietly got out of bed, and made her way to the wardrobe. She was careful not to squeak any floorboards. She pulled out her favorite emerald green dress and slipped it on. At her dressing table, she fastened her cloth buttons one by one, eyeing Ernest fast asleep in the reflection of the antique mirror. She remembered the night before. How she caressed his head, to help him sleep. He was so distraught. Her heart truly broke for him, it ached.

As she pinned back her curls, she studied herself. She really did look like her mum. Well what she knew of her from photographs. She placed a locket around her neck, in it a photo of her two childhood rabbits. They were each so round and lovely, tiny things. She missed them still, everyday. She floated around to the side of the bed and gently touched Ernest's forehead. He mumbled half asleep.

"You look nice Maeve, where are you headed?" He squinted through tired eyes.

"The print shop remember? Uncle Ben and I have business to take care of."

"Oh, that's right. Dear god, please don't let your ridiculous father become mayor. We will do everything we can. You have my support. I'm actually quite fond of this town." He grabbed her hand softly and gave a tired smile. His eyes were bright green today, flecks of gold danced in them as the sun crept through the curtains.

"Don't worry. Not on my watch. Thomas is taking over the inn again today. Don't feel like you have to go round to the graveyard today Ernest, maybe its too soon." She squeezed his hand. "Maybe give an update to James? Might make you feel a bit better to talk to an old friend." She slowly removed her hand from his grasp and caressed his cheek.

"I will do, thank you." He replied, as sleep began to pull him back in.

"Mhhm, get some more rest now. I'll see you later." She pulled herself away and tucked in the corners of the bed. She opened the curtains the slightest bit more, she hated to shut the sun out on the rare days it showed its face. Ernest groaned as he rolled back into the coziness of the duvet. Maeve made her way down the stairs and gingerly walked to the print shop. She didn't even manage to knock before Uncle Ben swung open the door. He shuffled her in and sat her down, he quickly handed her a cup of tea. His hair was wild, glasses crooked. He looked like he hadn't slept in ages.

"How's Ernest doing?" He asked as he disappeared into his photo room.

"He's still quite sad, a bit up and down really. He's stubborn though, so I think he'll end up sorting everything today. I told him not to feel pressured." She called after him. He came back out with a large blown up photograph.

"Ah that's good though, sometimes you have to take your mind off of things." He held the photo up toward the natural light, studying it with a hard gaze.

Maeve sipped her tea and nodded in agreement. "What do we have here?" She asked. Ben slowly flipped the large photograph around. Maeve's mouth was agape as she stared at what the image revealed. It was her father. His face severely angry. His hand was raised in a violent motion, while his other hand tugged harshly on a rope. A rope that was tightly attached to Wilbur's neck. She was dumbfounded. "He's a monster Uncle Ben..."

"And nobody is going to want a dog beating monster for mayor now are they?... I've been waiting to get something on him for ages Maeve. This could shut down everything he has. Not the inn, don't worry. That's yours. We will make sure of that." His eyes were alight with a crazed sense of justice as he continued to stare at the image.

Maeve felt vile. To be descended from such a heinous person. How had she managed to make it out alive? And as a rather stable and happy woman at that... Maybe it was best not to ask too many questions.

"We cannot post copies of that around town... its too soon... too graphic. Ernest won't be able to look at that. Not without starting a fight anyways." She urged, her brow furrowed heavily as she steadied her shaking hands on her teacup.

"No of course not! Charles would just rip them down anyways. I need you to draw it, make poster copies like you did before. Let's say 50? Can you do that?" Ben set the photo down in front of her. A look of determination crossed her face.

"Absolutely." She got up and immediately gathered her supplies and started the sketch.

"Great... I'll keep the original safe, in case anybody needs hard proof. The preliminaries start tomorrow... so we have to get a move on." He gathered up the original photo and placed it into a large envelope. He then slotted it behind some large reams of paper.

Maeve's arm started to cramp as she finished the final lines of the sketch. She wrote the damning words carefully along the bottom edge. "*Charles Livingston for Mayor?*" Uncle Ben excitedly came over, he slicked back his hair and lined up a ream of paper. He cranked the mimeograph to life as the horrid images were stamped out one after the other. Maeve's life flashed before her eyes as she thought of her childhood, the yelling, the absence of her mother and any love that could have come with her. The few times a year that Uncle Ben would visit... those were the only days when she had felt truly happy and safe. Her eyes misted over and the sadness turned to anger. Her skin went hot at the thought of this horrible man taking her peace once again.

Ben sat and stared at the pile of drawings. He looked up at her. She nodded with a fiery sureness. Swiftly, she grabbed every last one of the prints along with Uncle Ben's brown cloak which she effortlessly whisked around her shoulders. She pulled the hood around her face and looked over at her sweet Uncle. He gave her his biggest smile of approval. That was more than she needed.

"I love you Uncle Ben..." She said with a deep breath.

"I love you too Maevey. Always. Now go and paint the town red." He took a big sip of his tea and sat down proudly in his chair. Maeve nodded and walked out the door. In every mail slot of every home, in every store, and every bin, she slipped one of those drawings. With every one she let go, she felt herself become lighter.

When she arrived back at her cottage door she paused, there was a large hearse parked at the side. She reached out for the door knob, and a raven faintly croaked in the distance.

"The yew tree, the yew tree!" She paused and looked back, but the bird had vanished. She pondered it, and simply shook her head. As she opened the door, Ernest greeted her with the first genuinely happy smile she had seen in a long time.

"Hello there, I actually have good news." He said excitedly helping her with her cloak. "You may have seen the hearse outside! You're looking at the new and official undertaker of Asphodel on Eden. Lou was more than happy to have me on board." He beamed.

"That's lovely news! Only if you're sure you're ready. You don't have to rush you know."

"I know, I know. I just feel like its the right thing to do. It could help me take my mind off of it all. I think Wilbur would want me to keep going." He smiled at her again, and she could tell he meant it.

"Okay then, I guess its settled! I'm proud of you." She beamed. "Did you manage to call James?"

"Thanks Maeve, I really couldn't have done it without you and Ben." His smile faded a touch. "And I did call James, he was really quite sad about Wilbur. About me leaving as well, but he was happy too. He's always tried his best to be supportive. I made sure to tell him I'd like to keep in touch, and he agreed. He even arranged for some men to move my belongings over, friends of his." He reached over and hung her cloak neatly inside the cupboard door.

"That is really sweet of him. So it's official then?" She felt a cozy feeling spread through her.

"Absolutely! I am officially stationed here with you, if you'll still have me, and of course with Wilbur. I thought about what you said, and I'd really like to make a tradition out of the picnics. I know it isn't the same as having him here, but at least I get to see my boy. Just for a few moments." Ernest's eyes were getting teary again. She took her hand and placed it under his chin, she sweetly forced him to look at her.

"He is always close by Ernest." She looked deeply into his eyes, they had turned a darker shade of green. He nodded at her, and returned her soft gaze. She slowly released him, and made her way toward the kitchen.

"How did it go for you today anyway? Did you and Uncle Ben get that business taken care of?"

She looked back at him from the kitchen doorway, a fierce intensity bubbled through her. Ernest's face flashed a look of concern. "Trust me... he won't be mayor of this town. Not now, not ever. He'll probably be dragged out come tomorrow morning. If he's lucky." Her jaw clenched the slightest bit.

Ernest breathed a sigh of relief and followed her through to the kitchen. He lightly massaged her shoulders. "Thank goodness for that. What a nightmare. Are you okay though Maeve? Really okay?" He asked.

"I'm alright. I grew up with the man. I know how he is and what he is capable of. He needed to be stopped a long time ago. I just didn't have the courage, until now." She looked down and played with the hem of her dress. Ernest nodded sweetly.

"Let me make you a cup of tea." He gently lead her out of the kitchen and helped her into her velvet green reading chair. He returned moments later with two steaming cups of tea. They sat in silence for a while as the evening wind began to howl outside. It shook the fence and the surrounding trees. Maeve contemplated the depth of every change that had taken place in just one week. What was left to come. What was lost and what had yet to be discovered. She knew in that moment that Ernest's mind reflected her own.

"Even in the afterlife that wonderful dog of yours has saved our town." She looked at him, in the warm light of the woodburner, with confidence and a glint of mischief.

"That's Wilbur for you." His face lit up in a look of tender pride, but the yearning was still there. It would always be there. He went and placed some more wood on the fire, and it roared to life. Crackling warmth filled the cottage, it tickled the air with the sweet smell of cedar smoke. Maeve sat comfortably. She closed her eyes and heard Ernest boiling the kettle again.

"So when do you start your new job Ern?" She called sleepily.

"Tomorrow! I know it's soon, but I don't have much to lose. Lou said we can start off easy. He's real understanding."

"Mmmm... sounds like a plan. You should stop at the yew tree. Maybe on lunch or something." She mumbled, half asleep.

"Hmm? Why?" Ernest asked as he entered the room, but Maeve was fast asleep.

Chapter Twenty-Six

Pendle sat with Wilbur as the ceremony commenced. Pippin and Violet rushed in with hugs and words of encouragement. He could sense Wilbur's nerves even through the brave face he had put on. Nonetheless, he did feel quite proud of that daft dog. He had begun to warm up to the idea that, with help from his studious messenger, Wilbur might make a fine soul runner. He certainly couldn't herd sheep, but maybe he could herd the dead. Pendle snickered to himself.

He watched as Rell flew into the trees and came down with a collar of green satin. A small silver medallion dangled from the middle. It read "*Wilbur, Soul*

Runner of Asphodel." In exquisite lettering. Wilbur cautiously approached them, and the beautiful collar was placed delicately around his neck. Leer came around next with his blessing of herbs and smoke. After much ado, they looked to Pendle. It was his turn to approach the elders, and he was given his official messenger's medal. A baby blue satin ribbon this time, adorned with a medallion of white gold. It too stated his own name and position.

He watched as Pippin fumbled up the path next, rather like an erratic bumble bee. The tiny rabbit couldn't contain himself as he was presented with his official forest navigator hat, one fashioned in the style of 18th century explorers. Along with the piece de resistance, a golden compass, this was his medallion. Engraved all the same. It shun and danced in the light as Pippin twiddled it between his fluffy paws. The three of them lined up for their final blessings. Pendle looked to Wilbur, who gave him a worried but courageous nod. Leer and Rell spoke in one combined voice that sounded as though thunder had escaped from the heavens. The sun beams fell upon them in one perfect moment.

"We bestow upon you three, the key to Asphodel, to the afterlife. You move forward now and always with the duty of protecting each and every soul amongst these trees. With the intent of fulfilling their needs, and ferrying them through to their true purpose."

The three of them nodded and placed their paws into a well of deep purple mulberry ink. Carefully, they each placed a paw upon a letter of white birch. This was it. Pendle remained as still as stone. He took in the atmosphere one more time as the group slowly broke off. He sat tall and dignified among his friends and elders. After a time, he went over and gave genuine congratulations to Pippin and Wilbur who mused about their next adventures.

"I will see you all tomorrow, but I must be going to check on Ben. I haven't been home in a while. I'll check on Ernest for you Wilbur." Wilbur looked gratefully at him, and they all said their goodbyes. He respectfully bowed and then made his way into town. He slid his medal from his neck onto a hidden branch. Ben would ask too many questions. As he finally got into town's dark stone streets, something stung his nose. "Smoke?" He followed his nose past the print shop, toward the inn. The streets surrounding the inn were aglow with torch light. At least a hundred townspeople surrounded the inn. They all shouted for somebody named Charles. They were all waving large papers in the air. Pendle watched intently from the shadows.

"You'll never be mayor here!" Came an angry shout.

"You think this town is some kind of joke?!" Another furious voice reared up.

Then many voices in unison "We want you out!" Jeers and taunts flew from every which way. One of the large papers escaped someone's grip and landed gently in front of Pendle. He stared at it...

"Good god…" He murmured to himself as he took in the horrible image. The hairs along his spine tingled. Just then he saw a big man walk through the medieval doors of the inn. He spoke, and the lies fell deaf amongst the crowd.

"I am in no way any sort of abuser! This is a hideous lie." The man squawked, as he ripped down one of the posters from the outer wall of the inn.

"You're a hideous lie!" Someone shouted.

"Get him!!!" A wave of bodies lurched forward toward the angry man. Pendle's whiskers stood on end as he watched.

The man cowered further back against the wall. The crowd lunged forward again, but came to a halt as the man spoke once more.

"Fine… fine I concede! Take me away."

The crowd looked perplexed, as a horrible haunting laugh seeped from low in the man's belly. As he was pulled away from the inn, his laughter became maniacal. In one swift motion, he pulled an arm away, struck a match against the steps, and tossed it through the doors of the inn. It ignited quickly. His laugh now cascaded and scraped against the ancient stone. Hot red flames licked the windows, and reached up for the thatched roof. The crowd screamed. They viciously pulled down the heinous man, and dragged him as they ran. They eventually forced him to a stand and paraded him down the streets, and out of town. Pendle followed along the edges, until they finally threw him out of the gate. The sirens of the fire brigade wailed down the pitch black lanes. Pendle needed to warn Ben and fast.

Chapter Twenty-Seven

Wilbur awoke to the warm sun on his back. He laid out flat and stretched, as he turned over there was a small clink from his shiny silver tag. He felt Pippin and Violet nuzzled close at his side. Delicately, he stood and stretched out his stiffened legs. Pippin started to stir, but quickly returned to his dreams. Wilbur walked quietly out of the hollow and down to the river. He sat and pondered for a while. He wondered if he'd made the right choice. He stared down at the water. He studied his sparkling reflection in the morning light, and mused at the rays of sun that danced enchantingly off of his silver medal. He hoped his Ernest would be proud. His heart saddened to think he may never be able to show him what he'd done, what he had become. Slowly, he bent down to take a drink of the cool water.

As he lifted his head, a strange acrid smell filled his nose. Before he could figure it out, another reflection popped up next to his own. It was a tiny field mouse.

"Excuse me?" Came the incredibly small voice. He turned around to face the little creature. The mouse was now stood at his feet, he held what looked to be an umbrella made out of a leaf. He had the biggest ears Wilbur had ever seen, and a lightly singed yellow scarf wrapped tightly around his neck. He looked frightened.

"Hello there, are you okay?" Wilbur asked gently, he stepped back to get a better look.

"I'm not so sure really, my name is Alfred. I've lost my dad." He played with his scraggly whiskers.

"Oh, I'm sorry to hear that little one. Do you remember where you last saw him?" Wilbur laid down, hoping he would seem a bit less large.

"Well... last night we fled from the inn at the center of town. Our whole family did. The fire was so fast and so big." He spread his little arms out as wide as he could.

"Fire? At the inn?... Ernest." Wilbur got into a sit immediately, he sniffed the air. He stared worriedly in the direction of town.

"Yes... Um it's been put out now, but the place is destroyed... my home." He put his tiny umbrella down and nervously played with his scarf.

"I'm so sorry Alfred… it's just my best friend…" Wilbur could feel his legs shaking.

"Don't worry, it was late. Nobody was there, and nobody was staying the night either, we woulda seen em. No humans at least." He tried a reassuring smile for Wilbur.

"Oh, thank goodness for that…" He steadied himself. "More importantly, I'm sorry for what happened to you. That had to be frightening." Wilbur tried to relax his muscles. He didn't want to scare the poor thing anymore.

"It was… I'm not sure, but I might have lost everyone. I just want to find my dad." His little chocolate eyes began to well up.

"We'll find your dad for you little one." Wilbur gave him a comforting nod. His medal beamed.

"We will? I mean you'll help me?" His small face lit up.

"Of course, it actually happens to be my job. Well mine and Pippin's." He nodded toward the hill as a sleepy Pippin stumbled down in their direction.

"Oh, thank you! Thank you so much." His small chocolate chip eyes became a little bit brighter.

Pippin finally reached them and set out his map and compass. "We will get you sorted little friend! I'm Pippin, me and Wilbur, we're the soul runners." Pride oozed from his tiny voice.

"Soul runners?…That's silly. I'm still alive! I ran really quickly last night, the quickest ever." Alfred said puffing out his chest proudly. Wilbur shot a heartbroken look at Pippin. They locked eyes, and Pippin's gaze drifted to the singed scarf. His eyes glazed over.

Wilbur mouthed "Don't tell him..."

Pippin gave a hurried nod.

"Pippin... Where is Violet?" Wilbur changed the subject.

"Oh she's plaiting Leer's tail." He replied, and allowed himself to study the map again.

Wilbur just shook his head in amusement.

"Who is Violet?" Alfred asked sweetly, as he traced his little hands along the dirt.

"My sister, she's a ninny." Pippin replied studying his compass sternly. Alfred couldn't contain a little giggle, Wilbur again just gave a shake of his head and a sigh.

"I have a sister too... well actually 9 of them. Ninnies the lot of them. I hope maybe my dad and I can find them here too."

Wilbur glanced at Pippin once again... their eyes agreed to keep silent.

"Where's the last place you saw your dad Alfred?" Wilbur asked.

"As soon as we got out of the inn, we ran across the street, the one near here. Once I got to the otherside, I looked behind me and he wasn't there. I think I maybe fell asleep in the grass waiting because I don't remember much after that. I don't even know how I got across this river all by myself."

THE UNDERTAKER AND HIS DOG

"I'm guessing he is still on the other side of the river then. We'll have to help you cross over. Which means we'll need material. Boat material." Pippin put on his captain's hat and gazed across the river. "We best start now!" Pippin started slowly toward the riverbank, eyes to the ground. Alfred trailed excitedly at his heels.

"Pippin... um I could always just put you both on my back and swim across?" Wilbur suggested.

Pippin looked back disappointed. "Well that's not any fun is it?"

Wilbur rolled his eyes, and sniffed about for some large sticks. His nose took him all the way to the edge of the forest. The same eerie familiar feeling crept through him... as he peered through the trees he saw the yew tree. A small wreath lay on the ground nearby. His heart sank. As he walked further along the tree line, something peculiar happened. The yew tree began to glow. Wilbur stared, astonished... yellow light flooded from each crack where the hearse had hit. Surely he was imagining things. He didn't remember this happening before. Then, out of the corner of his eye, something black rolled into view. A hearse, a new one and in it... Ernest. The hearse slowed and parked right at the edge of the road. He could see Ernest through the windscreen. He held his head in his hands. He looked distraught. Wilbur's heart broke at the sight of his friend. All he wanted to do was to run to him.

His knees went weak at the final realization that he'd never be able to comfort Ernest again. The yew tree began to glow brighter and a deafening static-like noise began to fill his ears. He barked as loud as he could trying to get Ernest's attention. He wondered if he could see it too, but it was hopeless. He thought about trying to leave again... but it would never work. He had already made his vow. He took one last tearful look at Ernest. Then, fighting every last urge in his ghostly body, he turned away from him. His soul felt as if it would rip in two. He ran hard and fast, deep into the woods. He stopped and shook himself off. He shook and shook as if somehow it would shake the feeling away, this horrible yearning.

He knew he had to focus. Alfred needed him. He ran again, and tried his best to hold off the tears. He didn't look back. The voice of Leer echoed in his head. *You may only leave if it is on important business.* He shook his head in frustration. It wasn't fair. He wanted to help the lost ones, but he wanted Ernest. His heart couldn't choose which it wanted more. He wanted both. He longed for Ernest to see him now, but it was too late. As Wilbur reached the riverbank again, he heard a small voice calling out.

"Alfred! Alfred! I'm here can you see me?"

Wilbur could just make out another mouse on the far side of the river. He had a small hat on and carried a twig as a sort of walking stick.

"I'm here dad! I'm coming, I just can't get across this river." Alfred shouted back, his little toes were in the water. Wilbur noticed that Pippin was hard at work on a boat, but had made very little progress.

Wilbur sighed. "Bless him..." he said under his breath. He eyed a leaning tree further down the bank.

"Everybody watch out! Keep clear!" Wilbur shouted. Pippin heard him, he grabbed Alfred up and moved to the side. Wilbur ran to the tree at full speed, he climbed up it's sloped bark and began jumping up and down on it repeatedly. It snapped and creaked like ancient bones. His spectators watched in hopeful terror. The tree let out a huge groan as it came crashing down into the river below. Perfectly wedging itself between the banks. Wilbur rushed over to Pippin and Alfred.

"Right, Pippin, you walk behind Alfred as he crosses the tree, and I'll swim along the side, just in case."

Pippin nodded, a bit embarrassed as he remembered their last experience with the river. He held onto little Alfred's hand as they reached the tree. Slowly they began to walk across. Wilbur followed with a determined look and plunged into the chilling water. Alfred's father made his way to the opposite end of their newly made bridge. Wilbur fought the current as best he could. The water stung his eyes, and he spluttered. Once the end was in sight, a sharp squeak rang through the air. Wilbur turned to see that Alfred's foot had slipped, the tiny creature tumbled down the side of the tree.

He was hanging onto a small branch that jutted out from the tree. It bent dangerously under his tiny weight. Pippin's face went white. Wilbur pushed himself hard in their direction, he choked on the freezing water. He reached the edge of the fallen tree just in time. Alfred's little hands gave out and he tumbled down the side of the tree right onto the end of Wilbur's snout. His little round eyes stared into Wilbur's, horrified.

"Do not let go!" Wilbur gargled. Alfred nodded his head, his eyes full of fear. His little hands gripped Wilbur's jowls tightly. Pippin raced across the tree and down the bank on the other side. Alfred's father trailed worriedly at his heels. As Wilbur reached the bank, Pippin stretched out as far as he could and yanked Alfred up by the scarf. He held the little mouse tightly and ran him straight into his dad's arms. Wilbur clambered up the side and shook his fur out, panting hard. Before he turned to join everyone, he saw a small leaf emerge in front of him, he quickly dipped his nose back into the water, and pulled it out. He walked over to the others and daintily placed the leaf at Alfred's feet.

"My umbrella! Thank you, Wilbur." His small face beamed.

"Oh thank you, both of you." The old mouse wiped his tears with one arm as he hugged his son tightly with the other. Wilbur and Pippin nodded.

"Daddy aren't they amazing! They're heroes!" Alfred squealed.

"Indeed, they are." His father replied, peering sweetly through his microscopic glasses.

"Can we go and find mama and everyone else now?"

THE UNDERTAKER AND HIS DOG

A sombre look crossed the old mouse's face as he tried to find the right words. "We will son, but they aren't here. We can't stay here." He gave a concerned look to Wilbur who returned a reassuring nod.

"Where are they?" Alfred asked innocently. His father took a deep breath.

"Take my hand son, walk with me. I know just where they are." The tired old mouse tried on his best smile for his son. They joined hands and walked into the distance. They looked back at Wilbur and Pippin once more, and with a nod that could only mean thank you, they disappeared. Wilbur walked over and sat near the river. Quietly, he stared out. Pippin soon joined him.

"What's wrong Wilbur?" Pippin asked, he scooched closer.

"You always know..." Wilbur gave a soft smile. "I saw Ernest near the yew tree. He was upset... I don't think this sadness will ever leave him. Its clings to him like a leech. I can't bare it." He looked down at his paws. Pippin placed one small paw over his. "And the tree... it sounds crazy but it was glowing... I think I have to go back. I'm not sure why, but something is calling me back to that damned tree."

"That is odd... were you able to pass the tree line?" Pippin asked, he scratched at his ear.

"I didn't even try... I don't think there's any point. Leer said I can only leave again if it's for important business, but why on Earth was the tree glowing, Pippin?

That's what confuses me. It's like its taunting me. What could it mean?" Wilbur's face creased with thought.

"Wilbur... What does Ernest do again?"

"He's an undertaker."

"What are you?" Pippin asked with a sly smile.

"A soul runner...."

"What do soul runners do?" His little smile grew.

"Guide the souls of the..." Wilbur stopped. He looked down at Pippin who was quite proud of himself. Wilbur jolted up. "You are a genius Pip! I have to go... I'm sorry. I promise I'll hurry." He called as he started into a run.

Pippin smiled and put on his navigator hat with staunch confidence and called after him. "Go... I can hold down the fort Wilbs! Go get 'em. I'll see how Violet and Leer are getting on."

Wilbur gave his friend a trusting nod from afar as he reached the fallen tree bridge. His claws clacked against the bark and the dirt flew like fairy dust around him as he sprinted. He could hear thunderous wingbeats up above. The deep echo of Rell's voice rained around him.

"The path of a soul runner is never easy, but it is always his own."

As he reached the tree line, he skidded to a halt. The tree was no longer glowing, and the hearse was long gone. A cold feeling of disenchantment flooded through him.

"No... He'll be here." He told himself.

Ernest would come again. He knew he would. Wilbur was certain they both felt there was more to their story. He sat down at the edge of the wood, and he waited.

Chapter Twenty-Eight

Ernest parked the hearse at the graveyard, and Lou was stood in the gate, his plump frame and snow white hair were covered in mud. He put his shovel down and began to take off his soiled wellies. He gave Ernest a kind wave.

"See ya tomorrow Ern! Let me know if you need help down at the inn." The old man said in a sympathetic tone.

"Thanks Lou, I will. We'll see ya then."

As Ernest walked toward the cottage, images of the dreadful day before crashed around in his head. Ben crying at the door, Maeve falling to the ground in despair. The smell of smoke thick and harsh around them.

Sirens screaming through the air. His fruitless efforts to comfort Maeve. His blood felt cold. He wasn't sure what to do now, other than get his hands dirty. As he approached the inn, what was left of it, Maeve was already there. There were a few men from town with big push brooms clearing away the debris.

"Hey, are you okay?" Ernest asked softly. He put a kind hand on her shoulder. Her brown eyes glistened as they looked up at him. She forced a smile.

"I will be..." She leaned into his touch. They watched the workers for a while. "I have loads of savings, so at least I can afford to fix it back up. I think it's almost freeing in an odd way."

"What do you mean?"

"Well, this was always my dad's place. It just fell into my lap and I kept it going, but now is a chance for it to be mine. From the ground up. To erase him once and for all." Ernest gave her a tight squeeze. Her positivity never ceased to amaze him. "Where did you go yesterday, by the way? After work? I noticed you weren't at the cottage when I got back from Uncle Ben's." She looked up at him with concern.

"I just went and sat at the yew tree, I thought somehow I'd see Wilbur and it would make me feel better." Ernest replied, breaking their eye contact.

"I'm guessing he didn't show?" She asked, nervously biting at her lip.

"No, nothing." He gave Maeve another reassuring squeeze as he looked into the distance. He tried not to let himself tear up again.

"I'm sorry... I wouldn't give up Ern. I think you might be onto something about that tree."

"You think? Have you dreamt about it?" Ernest was hopeful.

"Since I met you... and yew trees are very special trees." Maeve replied with a slight smile, she held his hand and broke away from his hug. His heart became a bit more full. Maeve approached the foundation of the inn, arms crossed, and kicked a small pebble. She stared into the mess. Ernest noticed Uncle Ben walking up the street with Pendle close behind.

"Hello everyone! I have the plans here. Drawn by Maevey herself. I've already arranged for the builders. All in budget. Working sun up to sun down, 5 days a week. Any volunteers are always welcome." His presence was as calming as ever. He came closer and placed a large blue print on the old step. Everyone gathered around with oohs and ahhs. Ernest noticed Maeve's smile, a real one this time. Pendle walked around Ernest's ankles and purred.

"What are you going to call it Maeve?" A stranger piped up from the small crowd.

She gave an enticing pause. "The Ernest Collie." She said, turning toward Ernest with an endearing smile. Everyone's gaze followed. Tears bubbled up and rolled down his cheeks. He removed his flat cap and wiped his nose, he swiftly walked up to Maeve and pulled her in for a kiss. He could no longer contain himself. She melted into his arms, and he gracefully twirled her back to face the crowd.

She looked at them all with determination, hands on her hips. "Well what are we waiting for? Let's get started!"

The men laughed and resumed their positions. Ernest shared a big smile and a nod with Ben.

He walked over to the makeshift kitchen amongst the rubble. "Anybody for a brew?"

CHAPTER TWENTY-NINE

Wilbur had barely slept, he couldn't bring himself to take the chance. The morning came in dark and cloudy, and the air had cool and uninviting feel. The fog had rolled in thick and fast, and Wilbur frantically tried to get a glimpse of the sun. What time was it? Had he missed Ernest again? Would the fog block his vision? He approached the treeline and stared unblinking. He didn't know how long he'd have to wait, but he knew there was no other choice.

Whatever this tree was trying to tell him, he'd figure it out. One way or another. Every hair on his body told him it was something big. His eyes narrowed as he tried not to let a single blink overcome him. Eventually, his eyes started to sting and he allowed a himself very quick one. The fog shrouded the mighty yew tree in an unsettling grey veil. Wilbur's ears twitched as he heard what sounded like a car. Then around the corner came what looked like a large black automobile, he could barely make it out. It came to a slow stop at the edge of the field. Wilbur sniffed the air, and he knew it was Ernest.

"Ernest, please do not leave... please. Wait for me." He mumbled to himself. He eyed a fresh casket in the back of the hearse. He looked around worriedly at the trees. "What if this doesn't work?" He quickly shook the negativity off. "It will work." It had to work. As he looked around once more, a faint light seeped through the fog. The yew tree began its eerie glow once again. He shot a hopeful look at Ernest. He could barely see his face, but he knew this time, he saw it too. Wilbur took a deep breath and closed his eyes. He visualized the tree and its ghostly light. In the corner of his mind he could see the wisp, it too was fighting to get out. There could be only one. He took a few steps back and then ran forward with all his might, his eyes still closed tightly. "I'm coming Ernest."

A loud crack of thunder followed by a radiant explosion of light and Wilbur was gone. He felt as if he had disintegrated in an instant. He had become the mist. As he floated unseen toward the old yew tree, his breath was sucked away from him. The tree pulled him in with a merciless force, and with him came the wisp as well. It had been lurking, but who would emerge? What if neither of them made it? Within a few fleeting moments, Wilbur was pushed and pulled in every direction. His legs felt like they were being yanked off, but it didn't hurt. He was no longer of this world.

After what seemed like ages, he felt the hard ground materialize underneath him. He pummeled into the the dirt, head first, and scrambled to his feet. He was on the other side. He couldn't believe it, but he was now head on with Ernest and the hearse. Utter shock was all he could read on Ernest's face. Wilbur stumbled forward, he wagged his tail. Ernest finally closed his mouth and fumbled with the door handle. He leapt out and ran to Wilbur. They fell into the mist rolling and hugging. Ernest's face was streaked with happy tears. Wilbur couldn't control himself, he knocked Ernest over again and relentlessly licked his face. He felt Ernest push him off playfully and then wrap his arms fully around him in the tightest hug he'd ever received. They sat together in the wet grass.

"Wilbur... How? How did this happen? I knew it wasn't the end! I just knew it! But how?" The salty tears were streaked with dirt on Ernest's cold cheeks. Wilbur desperately wished he could talk to him and tell him everything, but he just forced his head underneath Ernest's arm instead. They sat there for a long time. Enjoying each other's presence once again.

"I'm guessing you still can't come home with me huh?" Ernest finally asked, he sniffled.

Wilbur stepped away slightly and looked at him, he shook his head.

"Right... I figured that. Is this the last time then? Or can we meet this way again?" Ernest's voice was filled with hope.

Wilbur looked at him sadly, he didn't know.

"I guess neither of us really know what's going on anymore do we?...Maybe we give it a try?" A heartfelt smile crept across his best friends face. Wilbur looked at him and gave an approving bark. He was glad Ernest understood him, without any words at all. He walked over to him and sat up straight. The straightest he'd ever sat. Finally, his friend noticed.

"What's this boy?" Ernest fingered the silver medal carefully, and read it aloud. "Soul Runner... Soul Runner? What is that? Where did this come from?"

Wilbur could see the confusion in his eyes. He ran around to the back of the hearse and barked over and over. Ernest came around and skeptically opened the boot to reveal the casket. He looked at Wilbur for further instruction. Wilbur barked again, he jumped in and out of the boot. Ernest was still confused. He jumped into the boot once more and shoved the casket lid to the side with his front paws, so it was opened just a crack. He saw that Ernest was watching in blatant bewilderment. He had removed his flat cap, his brow creased.

"Wilbur please don't scratch the casket. You know better than tha..."

His best friend paused. Dead silence, as light poured from the casket. It rumbled and shook. A ghostly figure rose from inside, the figure revealed a large man in a suit and tophat. He sat up and groaned as he climbed out of the boot. The man turned to Ernest first, who was flabbergasted. He looked as if he might faint.

"How do you do sir? Thank you ever so much for driving me." The spectral man's voice was kind and deep. Ernest's mouth was left agape. The man arched back, stretching himself out. Wilbur rushed over and gave Ernest's hand a reassuring nudge.

"And who might this be?" The ghostly man asked smiling down at Wilbur.

"Wil... Wilbur sir. " Ernest struggled for the words. Wilbur gave him a look to tell him to continue on, he sat up straight again to hint at his medal. Ernest gave him another look, this one felt like he was beginning to understand. Ernest continued shakily. "Your... uh... soul runner?" He looked over at Wilbur again for reassurance. Wilbur gave a nod.

"Ah yes! I've heard of such things. Not everyone is so fortunate to get a guide you know?" The man bent down to pat Wilbur's head. Ernest nodded in perplexed agreement. "Well lead the way then Wilbur, the afterlife awaits. Could you help me find my lost suitcase by any chance?"

Wilbur tried his best to bark a yes. He gave a wag of his tail. The man tipped his hat at him. Quickly, he ran back to Ernest and stood on his back legs. He rested his front paws on Ernest's chest.

"Wilbur this is incredible...I... " He decided to give up speaking, and gave Wilbur a nice scratch. Wilbur gave him one more kiss and got down. He started off toward the yew tree again with the man following leisurely behind. They disappeared into the ancient tree and were spat out nearer the treeline.

Ernest watched in amazement. "Uh... Same time tomorrow Wilbs? I guess?" Ernest called after him, half joking. Wilbur turned and barked a yes with a happy nod of his head. Ernest was stood in disbelief, his eyes as misty as the hills that surrounded him. "Right... same time tomorrow. I'll be sure to leave the caskets cracked for you from now on..." He laughed nervously and rubbed his forehead. "See ya tomorrow then!" Ernest's voice echoed a long the trees, sounding happier than Wilbur had heard it in a long time.

Wilbur sat at the treeline for a moment. The man waited patiently behind him. He stared longingly at Ernest, tail wagging as he watched him shut the boot and climb back into the hearse. He gave him one last loving wave as he turned the old automobile around. It drove away with a promising rumble. A promise of tomorrow, of a future for he and Ernest. They truly would always be together. In any life and in every death. A sense of peace that Wilbur had not known for so long, settled around him and throughout his ghostly frame. He turned to the man, the soul that needed him next, and they disappeared into the thick of the wood. He and Ernest had done it. They'd always be a team. A soul runner and his undertaker.

Chapter Thirty

Three months later...

Ernest walked quietly through the cottage in the twinkling light of dawn. He traced his fingers along the mantle piece, a large yew branch hung underneath. He gazed lovingly at his crumpled drawing of Wilbur which was now framed, taking up the center section above the mantle. He smiled.

"I wish you could see the new inn, Wilbs. It's gorgeous. Maybe the next equinox? Anyhow, I'll see ya later on for work." He chuckled as the disbelief washed over him again. He often wondered how any of this was real, but he didn't let the thoughts linger. It was all real and it was all good. He put on his tweed jacket and adjusted his flat cap.

"Hazel!... Hazel come!" Ernest called out as he patted his thigh. Within seconds a bumbling ball of black and white fluff rounded the corner. Ernest laughed as she skidded into his shoe. He bent down to pet her small fuzzy head. She gave a happy yip.

"Come on then, let's go to the inn and bring your mum a nice cup of tea, then we can see about introducing you to your brother. How does that sound? He's going to adore you. I just know it." He looked to the drawing of Wilbur one last time, and then looked down to see Hazel wagging her little tail in approval. Her eyes a rich deep brown, soft and familiar. He gave her a tender smile and grasped the warm cup of tea between his gloved hands. The cottage door creaked open, and they set off together, into the chilly autumn air.

ACKNOWLEDGMENTS

I'd like to say a heartfelt thank you to my family, friends, past teachers, and kind souls who encouraged me throughout this journey. A special thank you goes to my partner, Saul, for always helping me believe in myself and dissuading me from going insane during the rollercoaster that is book writing. Of course, my last thank you goes to Bruno, to whom this book is dedicated. The most wonderful dog a girl could ever ask for.

<3

ABOUT THE AUTHOR

Raven currently lives in Northern England with her partner, their four garden snails, and their two kittens. She enjoys anything to do with nature, animals, and the occult. This is her first novel, and was heavily inspired by her best friend and souldog Bruno. He has since passed away, but lives on in her heart and through her work. She hopes you, the reader, can find a bit of joy and comfort within this harrowing tale of Ernest and Wilbur.

Printed in Great Britain
by Amazon